Trust in the Lord with all thine heart;
and lean not unto thine own understanding.
In all thy ways acknowledge him,
and he shall direct thy paths.
—*Proverbs* 3:5–6

W0007174

MW0097 4957

To my wonderful readers.

Thank you for opening your hearts to my stories, and for allowing my characters to find a home with you.

Thanks also goes to my editor, Melissa Endlich, and my agent, Tamela Hancock Murray.

Words cannot fully capture the depth of my gratitude for their unwavering support and guidance throughout my writing journey. Their dedication, patience and insightful feedback have made this book a reality. For that, I am eternally grateful.

This book is as much theirs as it is mine. Thank you both for helping me bring my dreams to life.

Chapter One

She'd made a mistake. And she was going to die.

Florene Schroder lay on the hard, cold ground. Twisted and limp, she didn't move. Every inch of her ached. In her dazed state, she barely had the strength to move. Moments ago, her world had been a tempest of emotions. A heated argument with her boyfriend had escalated to the point of no return.

Scrunching her eyes shut, she fought to erase the memory of the assault. Visions of his open palm smashing against her face rewound and replayed in her mind. His rage and bitter accusations echoed in her ears. In a fit of anger, he'd stopped the car and yanked her out, kicking her aside like so much trash. She'd rolled over rocks and debris, landing at the bottom of a ditch.

Limbs turning slack, she struggled to remain conscious. A shiver ripped through her. Shock receded. The arctic wind turned sharp. Flecks of ice whipped around her, driving the cold deeper.

Hovering on the brink of hypothermia, she released a gasp of agony. Her mind raced with fear. Watching the vehicle's taillights disappear had frightened her more than the assault. Their fading glow was a stark reminder of her isolation. He'd left her in the middle of nowhere, miles from town.

Attempting to warm herself, she rolled over and curled into a tight ball. Clasping her hands together, she tucked them under her chin. She was cold. And so tired. Going to sleep, if only for a few minutes, would be so easy. If she slept, she could dream.

But if she slept, she would perish.

Adrenaline surged, and her eyes snapped open. Giving up would be fatal. Slowly, she uncurled. Clenching her teeth, she struggled to find her balance. A moan pushed past her lips. She had to get up and find shelter. Soon.

As she stood, her rebellious knees threatened to buckle. Drawing in a lungful of chilly air helped strengthen and steady her. Attempting to focus, she took one step forward, then another. Confusion wrapped around her like a blindfold, disorienting her senses. Rural highways were long, dark and endless. She didn't know where she was, or which way to go. On a stormy night, hours might pass before anyone came through.

Shivering, Florene crossed her arms to shield herself. Her thin jacket and jeans clung to her body, frozen and stiff, as if trying to suffocate her with their icy grip. Head tipping back, she focused on the angry sky. The clouds were thick and churning, sending down a fury that seemed almost sentient, as if nature conspired to punish her. The wind thrashed harder, merging the leaden flakes into a relentless whiteout. Unforgiving and merciless, the chilling blast seemed determined to swallow her.

As her strength ebbed away, exhaustion settled deep within her bones. Faced with an impossible challenge, she found a disquieting notion slithering into her brain.

Give up.

Eyelids growing heavy, Florene closed her eyes. It would be easy to slip into the dark void. Then she would be at peace.

A gentle flutter deep inside yanked her back from the precipice. If she died, she wouldn't be the only victim.

Crying in despair, she pressed her hands against her stomach. The revelation of her pregnancy had shaken her to the core. She might not care for herself, but what about the new life she carried? Every beat of her heart echoed with the realization that she was no longer alone; there was a soul, pure and innocent, relying on her every breath.

I have to be strong—for both of us.

A surge of determination strengthened her. *Ja,* she'd made mistakes. But the past was gone. Tomorrow offered the hope of forgiveness.

If she survived.

Exhausted beyond weariness, Florene peered across the highway, desperately searching for signs of human life. The frigid wasteland stretched far in every direction.

Focusing through the blur of whiteness, she struggled to make sense of the shifting landscape. Squinting hard, she glimpsed blocky shapes outlined amid a faraway gathering of trees. She couldn't be sure, but they looked like houses. A barn and other buildings, too. And was that firelight flickering through faraway windows?

Elation filled her. Her heart pounded with a mixture of hope and desperation. She couldn't be sure if her eyes were playing tricks, but the shapes grew more defined. The faraway farm beckoned, promising refuge from the merciless cold.

The squall gusted harder, giving her a nudge.

Breaths visible in the frosty air, Florene covered her belly, protecting the fragile life she carried from the storm's wrath. Driven by primal instinct, she began to walk, one leaden step leading to another...

Bundled in his heavy woolen coat and a wide-brimmed hat that shielded his face from the biting cold, Gilead Kestler trudged toward his *mamm*'s old farmhouse. The countryside was blanketed by a thick, pristine layer of snow. Each step he took consumed his boots. A trail of deep footprints followed in his wake.

As he sucked in breath after breath, the frigid air scorched his lungs. The chill seeped through the gaps in his coat, hurrying his steps. Reaching the front gate, he pushed it open. The hinges creaked, revealing a path he knew well. With its wooden beams and frosted windows, the rugged structure had easily fended off the storm. Puffs of smoke curled from the stone chimney, reassuring him all was well.

Struggling through the depths, Gil climbed the back steps. The enclosed porch was a welcome refuge, offering shelter. Stamping his feet, he gripped the frozen iron latch with his gloved hand and pushed it open. Given that the hour was early, he'd expected the kitchen to be cold and dark. It wasn't. A welcome rush of warmth enveloped him as he stepped inside. Kerosene lamps were lit, and the cookstove was stoked.

Mamm was up and hard at work. A variety of aromas mingled together: *kaffee* brewing in an old metal percolator, and the scent of bread baking in the oven

His brows shot high. *Mamm* wasn't supposed to be up. A few days ago, she'd injured herself while milking the cows. But now she stood at the counter, left foot heavily bandaged, and leaning on a cane to ease the pressure on her ankle as she sliced down a slab of bacon.

Gil hung his coat on a peg by the door. His battered hat followed. "What are you doing, *Mamm*?" he asked, wiping off the frost on his face. "The doctor told you to stay off your feet for at least a month."

"I've got no choice. Someone's got to keep this *familie* fed."

"You could have woken Nella or Eli."

"Couldn't ask either. They were up all night with the *boppli*. Isaiah's got the colic. He just settled down in the last hour."

Gil pursed his lips. Married ten months ago, Eli and Nella had recently become the proud parents of a baby *boi*. At first, the *boppli* seemed healthy enough. Lately, Isaiah was fussy and unsettled, given to long bouts of wailing. Caring for the inconsolable infant was difficult. The emotional toll was beginning to affect everyone.

"I'd have been glad to help." But he hadn't been asked. Moving into his grandparents' old *dawdi haus* to give the newlyweds more space had effectively isolated him from the rest of the *familie*.

"You need to have patience, Gilead. Isaiah's their first. Give them time to settle into their new lives."

Dropping his gaze, Gil shook his head. "Nella's never going to like me." He knew why, too. With his towering bulk and large hands, he didn't expect anyone to trust him to handle a tiny, fragile infant.

"There isn't anything Nella likes, so don't feel bad. Never met anyone so judgmental." Disapproval pursed *Mamm*'s lips. "Can't think why your *bruder* thought she'd make a *gut ehefrau*. But she's here and we have to make the best of it."

Rubbing a hand over his mouth, Gil suppressed his sigh. *Too bad the rest of us are stuck with her, too.*

Cane thumping the floor, Almeda tottered toward the stove. "Anyway, I can't stay in bed all morning when there's work to be done. This *haus* won't take care of itself." Despite her stubborn demeanor, the lines etched around her eyes and mouth revealed her discomfort.

"And you know I'll be glad to do the work." Closing the distance, Gil slipped an arm around his mother's shoulders. Spare and thin, there was almost nothing to her.

Mamm leaned against him, allowing him to bear her weight. "I could take a minute to rest."

Gil steered her toward the table and pulled out a chair. "You stay here." Waggling a finger, he added, "I mean it."

Mamm stretched out her leg to a more comfortable position. She sighed with relief as her discomfort eased. "*Danke*. I'll admit it feels *gut* to have the weight off."

Gil offered a sympathetic smile. Seeing her hobble like an invalid was heartbreaking. Still reeling from the tragedy that had befallen the *familie* when his *daed* passed, *Mamm* looked twice her age. She was clothed head to foot in black, and her hair was completely gray. An air of sadness hovered around her as she moved through the routine of daily life.

Satisfied *Mamm* was settled, he glanced toward the window. A frosty pattern adorned the glass pane, a testament to the frigid beauty of winter. The world outside was frozen solid. Driven by furious winds, the storm had already delivered a record amount of snow. Muted and gray clouds hung heavy and low. More was on the way. No doubt about it.

"I can't remember a winter ever being this severe," he said as he headed toward the stove. The rhythmic crackling of the burning logs was like a melodic lullaby. The metal percolator, also the relic of another era, perched atop the antiquated stovetop. The transparent knob at the top revealed the coffee's journey from clear water to the rich, dark brew that was a source of comfort. Steam wafted from the spout, carrying the promise of revitalization.

"Storms like this only come once a century," *Mamm* said, nodding with the knowledge of days gone by. "And when they do, they're guaranteed to be something folks remember for a long time."

Disappointment prodded hard. "Won't be making it to church this morning. It just keeps getting deeper." The bad weather meant missing the one time of the week he truly cherished. He enjoyed the singing of hymns, the comforting sermons, and the chance to renew his connection with the Lord. Texas wasn't famous for its snow and subzero conditions. But when the elements came together just right, the weather could turn brutal—and deadly.

"We'll make do with our own Bible reading today." Waving a hand, she added, "Check the *kaffee*, won't you? Don't scald the brew."

"I won't." Gripping the handle of the dented pot, he tilted it over the waiting cups. Taking each in hand, he returned to the table.

"Danke." Spooning in sugar and a splash of real cream, *Mamm* stirred the extra into hers. "Glad we laid in supplies," she continued after taking a sip.

Adding nothing to his, Gil swallowed a mouthful. "We'll be fine." Cords of wood were cut and stacked in the shed. Fruits and vegetables from the garden had been canned and preserved. Slabs of beef and bacon filled the smokehouse. Snug in their pens, the cows, goats and chickens would provide milk, butter and eggs.

Mamm shifted restlessly. "I need to finish my cooking. Can't just be sitting around doing nothing."

"You stay put. I can get breakfast on the table."

He set his *kaffee* aside and took up where she had left off, reaching for a cast-iron skillet hanging on the wall. Claiming the bacon *Mamm* had sliced, he forked it into the skillet. When the marbled fat connected with the hot iron, it released a hearty sizzle. He fetched a wooden bowl filled with fresh eggs and cracked a dozen before whisking them into a froth. Then, after adding a pinch of salt and pepper, he set the bowl aside.

"Peek at my bread, won't you? It should be about done."

"*Ja*, I will."

Gil grabbed a hot pad and pulled open the oven door. Fiery embers cast a glow on two perfectly browned loaves. Using a flat wooden paddle, he lifted each from the oven's depth. The mounds glistened with the subtle sheen of butter baked right into the crust.

"Looks *gut*," he said, placing both on the counter to cool. Returning to the bacon, he flipped the meat with a practiced touch. Next, he scrambled the eggs. Filling two plates, he then buttered thick slices of bread. Homemade strawberry jam and tall glasses of buttermilk rounded off the meal. Everything in its place, he sat down.

Mamm lowered her head, leading the morning grace. "*Danke*, Lord, for the food before us."

"Amen." Near starved, Gil was glad she'd kept it short. Fork in hand, he speared a mouthful of eggs. A bite of bacon followed. A hearty eater, he couldn't fill his stomach fast enough.

Mamm seemed to pick at her food. Her expression far away, she appeared lost in the tangle of her thoughts.

Gil wiped his mouth. "Something wrong?"

Mamm pursed her lips. "Guess you haven't decided on what I asked you about the other day?"

Gil's insides twisted. "You mean about giving my half of the land to Eli?"

"Ja."

Appetite fading, he nudged his plate aside. Silas Kestler had passed without a will. By law, the property belonged to his widow. The farm sat on a 120 acres of prime Texas land. Traditionally, the eldest *sohn* inherited the homestead. However, *Mamm* had recently asked him to lay aside his claim in favor of his younger *bruder*.

"Half and half would be fair," he mumbled. "That's the way *Daed* always said it should be."

"Silas said it when he was alive," she agreed. "But he's gone, *Gott* rest his soul. Eli's married now—and has Isaiah. He'll need more acreage to support a *familie*—and have something to leave his *youngies*."

Gil's heart sank. He knew exactly what she was saying and why. "And you're not thinking I'll ever have a *familie*?"

"I'm not saying it to be mean, Gilead. But you've always been...different. Nothing wrong with that, either. It's just the way the Lord made you."

Different. As in unacceptable, his mind filled in.

Mamm was right. He wasn't like regular people. Nearly seven feet tall, everything about him was big. Face weathered and rugged, he wore his imperfections like a shroud, believing his formidable appearance rendered him unmarriageable in the eyes of the young women in their Amish community. Because of his size, folks often treated him like he was slow-witted. The fact that he rarely spoke and kept to himself didn't help change any minds.

Gil fought to suppress his frown. "I hope you'll abide by *Daed*'s word, and not the bug Eli's put in your ear."

His mother returned a pleading look. "I'm trying to do the right thing."

"I've no say," he said, pushing away from the table. "The law says the property belongs to you. You're the only one who can settle it." They'd had this conversation before, and it always left a bitter taste in his mouth. "I've got work to do. Best get to it." Breakfast half eaten, he crossed the kitchen. Reclaiming his coat and hat, he headed back out into the chilly day.

Descending into silence, *Mamm* let him go.

Gil stepped outside and pulled the door shut. Exposed skin chilled within seconds, his breath cut a ragged gasp in the arctic air. The frost seeped through his coat and gloves, stiffening his joints. The day was as dark and gray as his mood.

Catching his hat before the breeze carried it

away, he lumbered forward. As a flurry of snow began to fall, he hurried his steps. The chaos of the storm threatened to return. A dismal winter stretched ahead.

Reaching the barn, Gil went inside. The odor of warm horseflesh, manure, leather tack and fresh hay all mingled together, assailing his nose. Secure in their stalls, the livestock shuffled, ready to be fed and watered.

Looking around, he felt a curious sensation wash over him. His stomach tightened with a nagging unease he couldn't identify. A shiver gripped his spine. But nothing seemed out of place.

Taking a cautious step, he reached for the pitchfork propped against the wall. He walked toward the haystack and came to a halt. Adrenaline immediately increased his heartbeat. Surprise was a gasp on his lips.

"What's going on ...?"

A pile of horse blankets lay on top of the thick straw. Under the lumpy mass, a pair of slender legs and bare feet stuck out...

Chapter Two

As her eyelids fluttered open, the first sensation Florene felt was a numbing cold that seemed to pierce every layer of her being. She was beneath some sort of blanket, shivering uncontrollably, disoriented and bewildered.

Pushing herself up, she wrapped her arms tightly around her stiff body. Her breath formed a foggy cloud in the frigid air, and her limbs ached.

Blinking away the blur distorting her vision, she attempted to make sense of her surroundings. She didn't know exactly where she was, but it all felt vaguely familiar. A multitude of scents tickled her nostrils. Wooden beams above her head creaked softly. Dim light filtered through the space, casting eerie shadows across the straw-covered floor.

A barn... She'd made it to a farm. The building didn't have heating, but it provided shelter, and that made all the difference.

Senses dulled by exhaustion, she had no idea how she'd made it to safety. The last thing she remembered was the bitter argument with Zane, on the side of a desolate highway. Slowly, distant memories of the swirling snow and her frantic struggle to escape its freezing clutches flooded back into her consciousness.

Florene's pulse quickened as a sense of vulnerability overwhelmed her. She felt isolated. Trapped.

Tears welled up in her eyes. In this strange place, she was a lost soul, a fragile survivor struggling to find her way.

The silence broke, filled by a man's voice.

"Ma'am? Are you all right?"

Heart missing a beat, she swiveled her head toward the stranger. She'd barely noticed the barn door swing open. Now a figure towered over her. Dressed in heavy winter clothes, the man easily filled every inch of the space he occupied. A heavy straw hat pulled low against the elements and a thick scarf obscured part of his face.

Tugging the old blanket closer, she gaped at the stranger. "Wh-who are you?"

The man approached cautiously, as if wary of frightening away a wounded animal. Pushing down his face covering and taking off his hat, he revealed his features. His hair fell in unruly waves around his face and shoulders.

"It's Gil. Gil Kestler." His deep, soothing voice contrasted with his intimidating appearance.

Thankfully, the name was one she recognized.

A silent, rugged presence in church and around town, Gil Kestler earned his living buying wild mustangs from the Navajo Nation in New Mexico, and breaking them for farm and ranch work. Customers who bought his horses believed they were the best to be owned. Nestled miles beyond Burr Oak, the Kestlers' homestead stood in tranquil isolation, far removed from the bustle of everyday life.

Florene released a deep sigh of relief, and the tightness in her chest loosened. "I know you," she whispered, voice barely more than a breath.

He grinned. "Most folks do."

She clawed strings of damp hair away from her face. "Don't you recognize me?"

Curious brown eyes searched for the answer. "You look like Samuel Schroder's youngest," he said after a long moment.

Relieved he'd made the connection, she nodded. "*Ja.* It's me. Florene."

Thick brows knitted. "Why, no one's seen you in—what?—two or three years?"

Tears welled in her eyes. "*Ja*, a long time…"

"No one knew where you went." Looking her over from head to foot, a grimace tugged at the corners of his mouth. "Something bad happened…"

Unable to acknowledge the truth, Florene lowered her head. She didn't need a mirror to know she was in terrible shape. The feel of bruises on her face and arms was something she'd grown used to. The pain would fade, but the memory would always linger, a phantom dancing on the edges of her consciousness. She wanted to speak, but the painful truth refused to pass her recalcitrant tongue.

"You're safe now." Slipping off his coat, Gil bent and wrapped it around her. "I'm going to take you to the *haus*. Is that okay? You need to warm up and get some food inside you."

She trembled from exhaustion, her eyes filling with tears. *"Danke."* A warm fire and hot drink would be welcome.

Attempting to stand, she stumbled. Strength depleted, her legs struggled to bear her weight. Dimly aware her feet were bare, she glanced down. Her tennis shoes were gone, but she didn't remember losing them. Somehow, she'd kept going, taking one painful step after another. The remnants of her thin jacket and torn jeans hung like a warrior's battle-worn armor. Determination to survive was the tool of her liberation.

"Let me." Without saying another word, Gil scooped her up. The floor beneath her disappeared.

Dizzy and disoriented, Florene wrapped her arms around his neck. The gentle way he held her was strangely reassuring. His large stride was deliberate and sure as he carried her outside. Driven by a gusty wind, the snow flurried with renewed vigor, painting the entire world white. The wind lashed at his enormous frame, but he pressed on without stumbling. Reaching the back entrance, he nudged open the door.

The kitchen was a stark contrast to the bitter cold outside, buzzing with activity. An older woman leaning on a cane stood in front of a wood-burning cookstove. A young woman holding an infant sat at the table, as did a younger man.

Passing them by, Gil hurried into the living room. A lounge near the hearth offered a cozy sanctuary. He bent and settled her onto its comforting cushions.

Gently reclaiming his damp coat, he replaced it with a blanket covering the back of the sofa. "That will help warm you," he said, tucking it around her.

Florene's shoulders slumped as she closed her eyes, letting the tension slowly drain from her body. *"Danke."* Old and well used, the chair was comfortable. Freezing and weak, she was thirstier and hungrier than she'd ever been in her life. Her insides twisted as her stomach gnawed at her backbone. She couldn't remember when she'd last eaten.

Glimpsing the newcomer, the older woman widened her eyes in surprise. "Oh, my! Who is this poor soul?"

Gil straightened to his full height. The top of his hat almost brushed the low beams of the ceiling. "It's Florene Schroder. I found her in the barn," he explained, filling in the details.

The older woman limped forward. Disbelief welled in her gaze. "Why, bless my soul, it is."

The younger woman at the table rose. "Bishop Harrison declared you missing years ago. No one knew where you went."

The younger fellow abandoned his breakfast, too. "He asked us all to pray you were *oll recht*."

Florene searched the surrounding faces. Recognition flashed across her mind's screen. Why, of course! She knew them all. The woman with the cane was Almeda Kestler, Gil's *mamm*. She also recognized his *bruder*, Eli. Happily, she knew the other woman, too. It was Nella Stutz. They were the same age and had gone to school together. Eli, a year ahead, was also in school at the same time she was. Gil was the only one she didn't know well. Nearly a decade older, he was almost grown and working with his horses by the time she'd started first grade. His *daed*, Silas Kestler, seemed to be the only one missing.

Hearing what they all had to say, she blinked back fresh tears. It only made sense no one knew what had happened to her. Zane's jealous nature allowed her no contact with her former community. At all.

"Your *familie* should know you're here," Almeda declared.

Gil glanced out a nearby window. "No one's

going anywhere today. Probably not tomorrow, either."

"He's right," Eli said. "They won't be clearing the highway for days."

"No other choice but to stay put," Nella added. Her tiny infant snuffled but didn't wake up.

"Can't call out, either. Lines to the shanty went down in the spring winds," Gil explained. "Phone company still hasn't gotten out here to repair it."

"Folks living outside town limits aren't a top priority for the county," Eli said.

Florene nodded. Even if she'd had a cell phone, she knew the signal wasn't always reliable. When nature unleashed its fury, farmers and ranchers living on the plains could be stranded for days. Having no electricity or phones often doubled the isolation of Plain folks. A hearty breed, time and experience had prepared them to survive.

As far as Zane knew, she was missing in the storm. Was he worried about her safety? Had he come back for her? Throwing her out of the car was surely an attempt to end her life. If he learned she was still breathing, she feared he might try to finish what he had started.

Dragging in a ragged breath, Florene squinted her eyes shut. *As much as I want to, I can't go home.* What terrified her even more was the thought that Zane might turn his fury toward her sisters and their husbands. He had met them and knew where they lived.

"P-please… Don't tell anyone." But if she couldn't go home, where could she go? Save for the scraps of clothes on her back, she had nothing.

"Why ever not?" Nella demanded. "Surely your *schwesters* deserve to know what's happened."

Florene shook her head. *"Nein,"* she said, switching to *Deitsch.* "I don't want anyone to know." Staying hidden would be the safest option. Her *familie* was innocent. She had no right to bring her darkness—her danger—into their lives. The thought of her loved ones being threatened because of her foolish actions twisted her stomach into painful knots.

Everyone exchanged glances. Silence stretched through a long minute, and then another. The burden she'd asked the Kestlers to shoulder was a heavy one.

Gil was the first to step up. "No one will bother you as long as you're on this property."

Florene blinked back tears. Woven with threads of genuine kindness and unwavering compassion, the empathy in his eyes touched a chord deep within her. She'd found not only shelter but also a glimmer of hope in the welcoming environment of simple Amish hospitality.

The dim light of the hearth cast flickering shadows on the walls, the snap of the fire punctuating the heavy silence. The room was tense, filled with the palpable worry that hung in the air.

Mug cradled between his hands, Gil had done his best to stay out of the way while *Mamm* tended Florene's injuries. He couldn't begin to imagine what had happened to her, but the experience had left her battered and broken. Instead, he focused on the present, hoping that the care they could offer would be enough.

Having fetched a bowl of warm water, clean rags and some salve made from healing herbs, *Mamm* worked tirelessly to mend what violence had shattered. "Someone made quite a mess of you, but this will help."

Florene winced. "I know I look bad."

"Bad doesn't describe it," Eli blurted from the kitchen table. "Looks like a horse dragged you a mile." Notorious for speaking his mind, he never failed to make his thoughts known.

Gil shot a narrow look at his brother. "Have a little sympathy. *Bitte?*"

"If you haven't got anything *gut* to say, then don't say nothing," *Mamm* scolded. "You can see with your own eyes she's been through trouble."

Looking between them, Eli shrugged, his brashness unyielding. "I'm just saying."

Jostled awake by the commotion filling the house, the *boppli* began to yowl.

Nella moaned. "Oh, not again." The lines on her face spoke of countless sleepless nights, and the circles under her eyes revealed the depth of her fatigue. Swathed in a blanket, Isaiah writhed uncomfortably, tiny face contorted with discomfort. His chest rose and fell with each labored breath. "There's too much excitement. He just can't settle down," Nella said when her baby filled the room with a shrill cry.

"Take him upstairs," Eli said. "Maybe rocking him in his bassinet will help."

"I'm so tired," Nella said, sighing heavily. "I think I'll have a little rest, too."

"I'll help you settle him." Giving the newcomer a wide berth, Eli led his *ehefrau* away.

Mamm ignored their complaints and dabbed the ointment on Florene's face. Passed down through generations, the salve was a family secret. "This will help you heal without leaving terrible scars."

"Danke," she said softly.

"Could have been worse," *Mamm* said. "You'd have frozen soon if Gil hadn't found you."

"It was *Gottes wille*," he mumbled, unwilling to accept praise. Helping another in need was the right thing to do.

"I'm grateful." Florene offered a wavering smile. "I'm just sorry it brings trouble to your door."

"No trouble to me," *Mamm* said and wiped her hands on a clean rag. "I'm just wondering how it found you."

Flinching a little, Florene visibly trembled, drawing the blanket closer around her shoulders.

Shame mixed with fright shadowed her taut features.

"It's all right," *Mamm* soothed. "If it's too hard to say, then don't."

Florene stared at the flames crackling in the hearth. Their glow cast gentle warmth throughout the room. "Zane Robbins did this to me."

"That *Englischer* everyone said you left with?"

"*Ja.*" Fear shimmered in Florene's eyes.

Mamm's gaze turned somber. "Your *schwesters* were heartbroken when you cut them off."

"I didn't do that by choice." Emotion tightened her throat, forcing a pause before she could continue. "After we moved to Dallas, Zane started changing, in the worst ways. It got bad, and I knew I had to leave."

Listening to her speak, Gil's stomach turned to knots. Most everyone believed the couple had eloped, but no one knew for sure.

Mamm reached for one of Florene's hands. "Go on."

"I told Zane I had money, in a bank account in Burr Oak. And if he would bring me to town, I'd be able to get it." Her voice cracked as she spoke. "I just wanted to get back home."

"Don't blame you one bit."

"I'd hoped we would make it before the storm got bad." Florene's trembling fingers brushed a tear away, only to have it instantly replaced by another. "We got in a fight again, and suddenly

I'd had enough. I told Zane I was leaving him, for good." She momentarily closed her eyes, as if seeking to ward off the memories. The bitter wind outside seemed to carry the echoes of her pain across the frozen landscape. "And then he slapped me and threw me out on the road. After that, he drove away."

"*Ach*, my *Gott*!" *Mamm* exclaimed.

Gil was no less horrified. Nor did he doubt a word, although in his sheltered world, such cruelty was unfathomable. He struggled to comprehend the darkness that existed in another human being. Marred by bruises, her face bore witness to the abuse.

"Any man who does that has no right to call himself such," he said quietly. A real man stood by his word, honored his commitments and faced the consequences of his actions. Only a coward would harm a woman or child.

Florene's gaze dropped, and her lower lip quivered. "I tried to defend myself," she whispered miserably. "But I couldn't…"

Mamm laid a hand on her shoulder. "Let your mind rest. What you need right now is something hot to drink and food in your belly."

"I'd like that," Florene murmured. *"Danke."*

Eli came down the stairs, walking with plodding steps. "Nella's finally got Isaiah to sleep."

"The colic should pass once he reaches two

months," *Mamm* said. "It's normal for newborns to fuss and cry. It'll pass, given time."

Eli offered a frazzled smile. His hair was disheveled, and weariness showed in his every movement. "Don't know how many more sleepless nights I can take."

"You had the colic, too. Can't tell you how many nights your *daed* and I walked the floor."

"Suppose I'll survive," Eli grumbled. "If I'd known babies were this troublesome, we'd have put it off a little longer."

"Don't get no choice when they come. When the Lord means for you to have them, He will send them."

Florene paled visibly. "You believe that's true?"

"Kinder sind unsere belohnung," Mamm said in *Deitsch*, eyes twinkling with pride. Isaiah was her first *enkel* and she expected many more in due time. "*Gott* says to fill our *haus* with them and we will be blessed."

Eli scratched his heavily bearded face with both hands. "Then I guess tired is blessed because that's definitely how I feel."

Gil shot his sibling a frown. If only Eli knew how lucky he was. He would have given anything for a chance to hug a *sohn* or *tochter*. He ached with a profound desire for an *ehefrau* and *youngies*. But the chance to marry seemed to have passed him by. Few women bothered to look past his towering frame and unkempt exterior. He believed—he'd heard many whispers describe him so behind his back—that he was a big, and ugly.

"Getting out and doing some work will surely wake you up," *Mamm* countered in her no-nonsense way. "Seems to me you could help your *bruder* with the chores. He's been handling everything while you and Nella slept in."

"Suppose I could." Grumbling under his breath, Eli reached for his coat and hat.

Gil claimed his own, slipping back into the layers of well-worn clothing. Despite Florene's unexpected arrival, there was still work to be done. Livestock needed to be watered and fed after a long, bitter night. The chores usually kept him busy until late in the day.

The brothers stepped outside, shutting the door behind them.

Face adorned with a scowl, Eli set his hat askew on his head. He'd buttoned his coat unevenly, a reflection of his resentment. A well-worn scarf was wrapped tightly around his neck. "Didn't know it was this bad. I hate the winter, being out in the cold." Eli had a wiry frame, closely cropped hair and skin leathery from days spent toiling in the fields. Freckles that seemed to multiply with every passing summer dotted his cheeks and nose.

Gil let the remarks pass. Eli complained about everything. All the time.

"It's a *gut* thing you found her when you did,"

his *bruder* continued, stamping his way through the snow. "Another half hour and she probably wouldn't have made it."

"She's lucky she survived. *Gott* was looking out for her last night."

"Don't know how sorry I feel for her." Eli sniffed as they shuffled toward the barn. The flurries, now falling fast, frosted his beard with glistening crystals. "Everybody knows *Englischers* are trouble."

"A lot of them are decent folk, trying to live honest lives."

Eli's eyes narrowed. "Decent or not, they are not *our* kind. We don't need their ways fouling our minds and our traditions," he snorted as his brow furrowed beneath the brim of his hat. "Florene should have known better to commingle with one. Can't say she wasn't warned, either."

Lips going flat, Gil turned his head. The conversation was a challenging one, and he wasn't one to point fingers or spread gossip. Keeping his thoughts to himself, he rarely spoke unless spoken to. Still, he had two good ears, and he often overhead things best left unsaid. The Amish were human, after all. Tongues often set to wagging when a member of the community strayed into unrighteousness. The secular world was a temptation many Plain youths had a hard time navigating. Lured by *Englisch* ways, Florene had made a dreadful mistake. She'd paid for it, too.

Spirit as battered as her body, the poor girl needed the comfort of her own people. Born Amish, she was still part of the flock. And just as the Lord gathered the lambs in His arms, it was up to them to offer sanctuary to the lost. But that had always been the way Plain folks were. They looked out for one another.

Though the immediate crisis had passed, Gil couldn't shake the sense of foreboding that nagged him. Florene might be out of danger now, but he suspected her troubles were far from over.

Chapter Three

Florene looked at the dress laid out on the bed. Modest, with a high neckline and long sleeves, and the material a rich shade of blue. A white apron, freshly starched, lay beside it, in addition to a prayer *kapp*, also white and crisp.

"They should fit all right," Almeda Kestler said. "You and Nella are about the same size."

She picked up the frock, pressing it against her body. "I haven't worn Amish clothes in so long."

"Got no choice. What you're wearing is rags."

That was true. When Zane kicked her out of the car, all she had were the clothes on her back. The personal items she'd packed for the trip were still in a backpack in the trunk of his car. Not that it mattered. He hadn't allowed her to have much of anything.

She laid the dress back across the bed. "I suppose you're right."

"I'll let you get cleaned up." Leaning on her cane, Almeda hobbled toward the door. Her movements were painful, and she winced a little as she walked. Still, she hadn't voiced a single complaint, bearing her affliction with silence and grace. "Come down to the kitchen when you're ready."

"*Ja*. I will."

Closing the door, the older woman departed.

Left alone, Florene breathed a sigh of relief. The guest room was a peaceful sanctuary: a flickering oil lamp cast a gentle, warm light and scented the air with the faint aroma of kerosene. A hand-stitched quilt adorned the bed, and each piece of furniture in the room was made from rich, dark wood, showcasing commitment and craftsmanship. The simplicity and functionality of the space was also free from the distractions of modern technology. Instead of a television, a large picture window offered a breathtaking view of the vast farmland swathed beneath a deep layer of snow.

The old farmhouse had no electricity. Thankfully, it had an indoor bathroom and running water—but that didn't extend to the second floor. For convenience, a washstand with a basin and pitcher stood near an armoire, allowing one to wash and dress in privacy. Amusingly, there was also a chamber pot.

A chuckle slipped past her lips. Stepping into an Amish home was like stepping back into the past. In the Plain world, time moved at a different pace. The daily routines, rooted in tradition and faith, provided a sense of stability and purpose. Farmers plowed their fields with horses, eschewing tractors and machinery. Meals were a communal event, a time for *familie* to gather around a table laden with the fruits of their labor. The click-clack of sewing machines and the sound of horse-drawn buggies were the soundtrack of their existence.

Since her *rumspringa*, she'd turned away from old-fashioned traditions, wearing trendy clothes and cosmetics, and living a life that most Amish frowned down upon. Eagerly grasping the forbidden fruit, she'd taken a hearty bite. But the *Englisch* world had turned out to be a mirage. A trap filled with lies and deceit.

And it had all nearly claimed her life.

What she'd once believed to be an annoyance and limitation, she now longed to rejoin. She wanted to come back to her birthright. Not only for herself, but for her unborn child.

Thinking of her *boppli*, she instinctively cradled the gentle curve of her belly. Close to the end of her fourth month, her thickening waist would soon reveal her secret.

Shame slithered in. She'd once derided her sisters for aspiring to be wives and mothers. The words she'd mocked them with echoed through her mind, returning to haunt her. Regret tasted bitter in her mouth. She longed to apologize, to find a way to make amends and heal the hurt she'd caused.

But that wasn't possible. She couldn't go home. Not now. Maybe never. She wasn't even sure she could be Amish again. It was possible the community and church wouldn't even want her back. Pregnant. Unwed. A sinner, for sure. What did she have to offer? Nothing.

Lost and floundering, she clenched her hands together, sending out a silent plea of desperation. *How do I fix this mess?*

She didn't know. But she hoped answers would come. Soon.

The blizzard had brought everything to a standstill. Frozen in solitude and silence, the remote farm was the perfect place to disappear without a trace, a haven where she could heal. It wasn't a permanent arrangement. However, it would give her time to think, sort through her thoughts and plan a future. She needed to think long and hard. Did she want the baby or not?

With a determined sigh, Florene turned away from the window. The creak of the old wooden floorboards beneath her bare feet was like a battle cry, a declaration of her resolve to find a future worth living.

Moving to the washstand, she poured water from the pitcher into the basin. She splashed it on her face, letting it purify not only her skin but also her troubled thoughts. The droplets fell from her cheeks like tears, mingling with the unspoken fears haunting her for months. The mirror over the basin showed a woman who seemed like a stranger, a woman torn between the past and an uncertain future. Her bruised face spoke of the trials she had encountered on her journey away from the community. She wondered if the Lord would forgive her for straying from the path, for the choices she had made—and for the life growing within her.

Ready to dress, Florene found her hands trembling as she reached for the simple garments Almeda had given her. She slipped the dress over her head, the material settling gracefully around her burgeoning figure. As she adjusted her attire, she couldn't help but notice it felt like a second skin—a part of her she'd tried to shed but was now being forced to reconsider. The calf-length outfit, modest in every way, bore no frills. Handmade practicality adorned every stitch.

Fastening the snaps, she added the white apron around her waist, tying it securely in place. As her fingers worked the knot, the weight of tradition settled on her shoulders. Black stockings were next, soft and warm against the chill of the room. She rolled them up her legs and slipped her feet into a borrowed pair of simple black leather boots before pulling the laces tight. The fit wasn't perfect. But it was close enough.

Last was the prayer *kapp*.

Florene picked it up. Her hands trembled as she held it, memories flooding back—of peaceful Sundays attending church, of the comforting rhythm of hymns and the reassuring presence of her *familie* by her side. But her hair was an unruly obstacle, hanging in wild disarray around her shoulders. It wouldn't be right to put the *kapp* on over that mess.

Gathering her courage, she stepped out of her room. Following a short hall, she walked down creaking wooden stairs into the spacious living area on the first floor.

Almeda and Nella were in the kitchen. The older woman fed her fussy grandchild while her daughter-in-law tended the morning chores. Thankfully, the men hadn't yet returned from their work outside.

"*Ach*, you look better," Almeda greeted, eyeing her from head to foot.

Turning away from the sink, Nella wiped her hands on a dishcloth. "Oh, *gut*. I see the clothes fit."

Florene gave her school chum a grateful look. When they were younger, they'd been close. Their bond had grown strained as their paths had diverged. She'd left behind the simplicity of Plain life. Nella Stutz remained firmly rooted in the close-knit community. Their friendship had ended in distance and silence.

Despite the rift, Florene was grateful a flicker

of their association remained. "*Danke* for loaning me some clothes. I appreciate it."

Nella smiled warmly. "You are welcome."

"Could I ask you to help me neaten my hair and put on my *kapp*?"

"Oh, my, I'd be happy to!" Nella clapped her hands, blue eyes sparkling with animation. Pointing to a chair, she continued. "Sit there while I get a few things to fix your hair."

Florene obeyed. Feeling more than a little out of place, she folded her hands in her lap. An uncomfortable silence stretched on. She knew these people because they shared the social connections of church and community. But she also didn't, because of her time away.

I have nowhere else to go, she reminded herself. She'd best start figuring out how to fit back in.

She glanced toward Almeda. Finished feeding the *boppli*, the older woman raised her grandson to her shoulder. She patted his back with a firm hand. The infant released a hearty burp.

"There we go, little one," she soothed. "You'll feel better now."

Watching grandmother and grandson together, Florene wondered what it would be like to rock her *kind* in a handmade wooden cradle. It was easy to imagine softly singing lullabies passed down through generations. Other women in the community were always ready to lend a helping hand with little ones. They came together to celebrate the joys of motherhood, happily knitting blankets and sewing clothes that would keep *youngies* warm in the winter.

"How old is he?"

"Isaiah's six weeks." Almeda beamed with pride. "Nella and Eli married before the spring planting, so he's about right on time."

"I never imagined she'd marry Eli," she confessed. Rangy and thin as a youth, he was not a handsome teenager. Time had changed that. Eli had turned into a fine man. Tall as he was, though, he wasn't half as big as his older *bruder.*

"I'm happy Eli settled on a *fraa.*" Almeda lowered the infant from her shoulder. Tucking the folds of his blanket around his fragile body, she rocked him gently. The little one responded with a gurgle of contentment. For the moment, he was quiet. "Time was getting away."

"And Gil?" she asked.

"Nein." The older woman released a distressed sigh. "Gilead is a *gut* man, but he wasn't blessed with fine manners or a charming smile." Consternation etched her forehead, deepening the lines on her face.

Florene sensed Almeda was worried about her eldest *sohn*'s future. Amish mothers prayed for their *kinder* to find loving partners and build *families* of their own.

"When the time is right, Gil will find the love

he deserves," Florene said, trying to offer comfort and hope without causing unintended offense.

Almeda nodded gratefully. "I pray you're right."

Nella breezed back with a few things in hand. "I've got everything I need to fix you up right," she announced, waving a brush, comb and a pair of scissors.

Florene sat still as the comb pulled out tangle after tangle. The breakage was bad, leaving ragged, uneven edges.

Nella snipped with gentle precision. "I'm sorry I'm having to cut so much. But it's been bleached, and it's falling out." Normally, the *Ordnung* didn't encourage women to cut their hair. But there were exceptions allowed for the care and tending of damaged tresses because of illness or other circumstances.

"Cut away all the damage," Almeda advised. "That's the best thing."

Florene felt her throat squeeze. She inwardly winced as inch after inch disappeared. "It's all right. It'll grow back."

"It's not too bad." Fluffing and arranging the shorter, chin-length bob, Nella sat the starched white *kapp* into place, securing it with pins. She adjusted it with care, ensuring it sat perfectly straight. "Now you look like you did back in school," she said, stepping back to survey her work. "You always were the pretty one."

"Danke." Florene raised a hand, running the

tips of her fingers along the stiff edges. It felt strange yet oddly comforting to have her hair concealed once more, a symbol of humility Plain women willingly accepted. Returning to a life she'd left behind, this act of dressing was more than just donning clothing—it was a reconnection to her roots and her identity.

Only one thing eluded her.

Faith.

With a practiced motion, Gil grasped the twine binding a bale of hay. Hoisting it onto his shoulder, he barely felt its weight as he walked toward the corral where the wild horses waited. Magnificent creatures with flowing manes, the animals nervously stamped their hooves. A few nickered impatiently, their warm breath forming puffs of steam.

Eli walked ahead and pushed open the gate so they could reach the feeding stations. Positioned behind a line of trees that helped break the intense wind, simple three-sided sheds provided adequate shelter for the herd. Half a dozen lean-tos were big enough for four horses apiece. Altogether, the corral housed two dozen. A hearty breed, the animals were equipped to handle the cold weather as long as they had shelter. Their thick winter coats added an extra layer of protection.

Gil heaved the bale into a trough. Snapping the twine binding, he spread it out.

"There, there, I didn't forget you." Hay spread, he uncovered pails of oats and other forage to add to the horses' diets. The rhythmic sound of the animals munching their breakfast filled the air. He next checked the water, shattering the thin layer of ice that had formed on the surface. A battery-powered heating element prevented the liquid in the trough from freezing through.

Eli frowned with disapproval. "You talk to them like they understand." Annoyance flickered in his gaze as he looked the animals over. As always, he did more watching than working.

"They do." Satisfied the horses were sound, Gil reached out to pet a favorite mare. Her coat was thick, and she nuzzled him affectionately. Before the weather turned bad, he'd been working on breaking her for the saddle. The animal had responded well. Once fully tamed, she would be ready for sale.

Be hard to let this one go. He'd thought about keeping her for the farm. Broken right, she'd make a fine plow horse.

"Doubtful, but whatever." Shivering, Eli burrowed deeper into his coat. "Can't say I like this cold. The only *gut* thing about it is spring planting will be a lot easier." Despite his best efforts, last year's growing season had been a disappointment. The summer had been unforgivingly dry, and lack of rain had withered the fields. The corn, once tall and proud, stood stunted and parched, and the drought tolerant sorghum had yielded only a meager harvest. The weather had taken a hard toll on farmers, delivering heartache and worry to many who depended on the crops to make their living.

Rubbing his hands together to ease the ache of the cold in his fingers, Gil nodded. "I'm praying the Lord sends more." The heavy snowfall, a rarity in the region, was a blessing. The deep blanket of snow would insulate the soil, preserving the precious moisture. It was a reminder the earth had its seasons, and every season had its purpose.

Eli gave the swirling flakes a baleful look. "Don't think you need to do that. It'll take at least a week for this to thaw. Maybe longer." His breath was a frosty plume around his face.

"I don't mind it. Makes the world look prettier if you ask me." Giving the mare a last pat, Gil stomped away from the shelter. Struggling through the deep snow, he meticulously inspected the fencing. A single flaw in the corral's defenses could spell disaster for the horses. Coyotes were vicious predators and penned livestock were easy prey. Driven by hunger and desperation, the pack would attack the defenseless animals without mercy.

Eli grew impatient. "Can we go?"

Gil trudged toward the gate to join him. "*Ja*. I'm coming." The morning's work was hardly finished. The animals in the stables needed to be taken care of, too. He'd meant to do that first thing but finding an unexpected visitor had thrown him off schedule.

Despite its worn appearance, the barn was a haven of warmth and life. Cows, their brown eyes wise and gentle, occupied one corner, occasionally lowing softly. The rabbits huddled together in their cages, their soft fur forming a mosaic of grays and browns. The chickens, too, were secure in their coops. At the far end were the horses that did the hard work. Powerful and majestic, they pulled heavy farm machinery.

Relieved to be out of the cold, Gil reached for a pitchfork. He mucked out one stall, his movements precise and methodical.

Eli pushed the wheelbarrow up for him to fill. "Don't suppose you've got an answer about expanding our cultivated acreage?"

Gil barely glanced up. He'd known by the look on his face that Eli had something on his mind. That, and the fact *Mamm* had already had her say at breakfast.

"My answer's the same."

Eli let the wheelbarrow drop. "All you do is use the land for forage. It's just sitting there, going to waste."

"The horses need the space."

"The acreage I've got is limited," Eli said, pressing harder. "With each season, it takes more to make ends meet. Doubling my planting would increase my chances for a better profit."

Standing straight, Gil leaned against his pitch-fork. "Maybe it would. But without the horses, we wouldn't have anything to fall back on."

It was true. The income he made from the sale of the horses gave the *familie* a cushion when times were hard. The Amish were thrifty folks, but they still had bills. Even if a man owned his land, there were still taxes, along with equipment to be bought and maintained. There were also other living expenses, such as *Mamm*'s trip to the emergency room. Plain folks didn't have health insurance, and most paid out of pocket when seeing a physician. It still took cash in hand to settle a fair debt.

Eli flinched. "I'm aware. And I thank you for carrying us. I pray you won't have to do it next year, or any other year."

"I will if I have to," he said. "You know that."

"I need more land," Eli blurted.

Gil huffed. "Doubling the acreage doubles the work. And Isaiah has some growing to do before he's big enough for the fields. And I'm no farmer."

"True. But he won't be little forever. Time will pass. And the Lord will surely send more *youngies*."

Gil offered a thin smile. "Surely."

"A man should think about the future." Eli's brow furrowed, and a mix of worry and anticipation darkened his gaze. "If I had the money, I'd buy more land outright."

Gil pushed out a sigh. On one hand, he understood his brother's concerns. A farmer's prayer for a bountiful harvest wasn't always granted. The more acreage planted, the better chance of success. But it could also double the loss if the crops failed.

"It's not my decision, one way or the other," he said.

Eli pursed his lips. "Guess not."

Reaching a mutual impasse, they returned to work in silence.

After a grueling morning, their hands numb and their faces reddened by the cold, the brothers finally made their way back to the farmhouse. Shaking off the snow from their clothes, they shed their damp outer layers. Their coats were hung on pegs by the back door to dry.

Haus tidy, the women were settled in the living room. After the chores were done, Sundays were devoted to church, socializing, and other quiet pursuits. *Mamm* sat in a comfortable chair, resting her tired bones. Nella sat on the sofa, rocking Isaiah, who was, thankfully, sleeping peacefully in his bassinet.

Gil's gaze shifted toward the narrow love seat. Outfitted in Amish clothing, Florene looked entirely different. She was clad in a blue dress, and her hair peeked out from beneath the edges of her *kapp*, framing her delicate face. The *familie* Bible lay open on her lap.

His mouth went dry, and his heart skipped a beat. Despite the bruises marring her face, she was a vision of purity and grace. The nearby hearth lent her skin a rosy glow, a stark contrast to the pallor he'd seen when he'd first rescued her. In her new attire, she looked like she belonged right where she sat. He wanted to say something, tell Florene how pretty she looked, but words escaped him.

"We can't get to town for church, so we're having Bible study before lunch," *Mamm* said.

"I was hoping we'd eat first," Eli grumbled complainingly. "I'm starved."

Mamm smacked him with a frown. "Your stomach can wait, Eli," she fussed. "*Gottesschwert* comes first in this *haus*."

"We're having ham sandwiches. There'll be apple pie, too," Nella chimed in to placate her fussy *ehmann*.

Eli raised his hands in surrender. "At least let me get something hot to drink. I'm about frozen to the bone." He poured himself a cup of *kaffee* from the pot on the stove and joined his wife.

Gil looked around for a place to sit. Every seat was filled save for the space beside Florene. Unsure she would welcome his company, he hesitated.

Mamm pointed toward the kitchen table. "Pull up a chair so you can hear."

Gil did as he was told. Placing the chair near

the love seat, he sat. "You look much better," he said, attempting to be welcoming.

A faint blush touched Florene's cheeks. "*Danke* for your kind words—and your kindness. I appreciate all you've done."

Suddenly tongue-tied, Gil cleared his throat. "What were you reading?"

"Almeda asked me to read from Romans," she said.

Mamm leaned forward. "It was something I felt Florene needed to read today. It reminds us that nothing can separate the children of *Gott* from His love."

Florene looked down, her fingers nervously worrying the edge of one page. "I haven't done this in a long time. Bear with me if I stumble."

One thing Gil enjoyed most about church was listening to the gospels. The Holy Scripture never failed to bring a deep sense of comfort. "Please go on."

Discomfort momentarily darkened Florene's expression. "I'm not sure I—" Suddenly flustered, she thrust the heavy Bible toward him. "Why don't you read for us?"

Surprised by her offer, Gil mutely shook his head.

Looking between them, Eli snorted with derision. "Won't do any *gut* to hand it to him."

"It's true," Nella added. "He can barely read."

Eli's smirk widened. "His body outgrew his

brain," he said, pushing the verbal thorn deeper. "He's no smarter than a rock."

Mamm frowned in his defense. "Hush, both of you! It isn't anything to make fun of."

Too late. The damage was done.

Heat crept into Gil's face. Belonging to a community where knowledge was cherished, he found his inability to read a heavy burden to bear. His eyes usually wandered over the pages as he attempted to make sense of words. But he could comprehend only a few. Knowing this, *Mamm* assisted him in deciphering important letters or documents that came his way.

The room fell silent, save for the crackling of the fire in the hearth. A long minute ticked by, and then another. The embarrassment became too much to bear.

Gil pushed his chair back with a harsh scrape against the wooden floor. "I need to check the gate on the corral. Think I forgot to lock it." Then he fled, leaving the warm cocoon of the family circle.

Pausing only to grab his coat and hat, he headed back out into the storm. He stumbled through the snow as his mind whirled. A guttural groan of frustration, anger and shame passed through his lips. Eli never failed to remind him he'd never fit in. That he'd never belonged in the *familie* because he wasn't right in the head. Always on the outside looking in, he felt so alone.

Why did you make me this way, Lord? He clenched his hands tightly, as if trying to grasp on to some semblance of purpose and meaning. But it did no good.

He was nothing. Nothing at all.

Just a big, dumb lug nobody wanted.

Chapter Four

The scent of a hearty lunch—a simple yet satisfying meal prepared with care—filled the air.

Florene couldn't ignore the pit in her stomach
as she sat at the kitchen table. Though starved
when she'd arrived, she'd barely taken a single
bite. The incident between Gil and his brother
was still very much on her mind. The unkind-
ness from Eli made her uneasy.

Should I say something?

No. It wasn't her place. The Kestlers had given
her shelter when she needed it most. In the Amish
community, such gestures were not to be taken
lightly. The *familie* had taken her in without hesitation, giving her a roof over her head and a seat
at their table.

Despite their hospitality, the atmosphere in
the house was not a warm one. An undercurrent
of tension thrummed between Almeda and Eli.
The storm outside seemed to have found a mirror within the confines of the home.

The food was consumed in silence. Only Eli

seemed to be unaffected by the awkward exchange. Eating with gusto, he'd even helped himself to a second slice of apple pie topped with scoops of vanilla ice cream from the hand-cranked churn.

Almeda launched a frown of disapproval toward his overflowing plate. "Two servings is enough," she warned. "I'm saving that last slice for your *bruder*."

Eli brushed her off, digging his fork into the dessert. "Gil should come and get it if he wants it." Popping the bite into his mouth, he swallowed it. "Not my fault if he's going to sulk."

"You didn't have to be so unkind," Almeda returned.

Eli shrugged. "Gil will get over it. He always does."

Nella gave her *ehmann* a look. "It was mean of us to tease." She glanced toward Florene. "Not a lot of people know Gil can't read."

Florene politely folded her linen napkin, laying it aside. No use trying to eat. Her appetite had vanished. "I had no idea."

"Now, that's not true," Almeda said. "Gil can read a little. It's just the big words that get the better of him."

"He never was right in the head," Eli snorted. "All he thinks about are those horses."

Almeda paled visibly. "You don't know what you're saying, *sohn*." Shadows of sorrow enhanced the lines around her eyes and mouth. "There's no reason to be mean. Just let it go. Please."

Eli didn't. "Think about it. Gil's tying up acreage I could be planting and harvesting."

The old woman pursed her lips. "Don't start pushing."

"I have every right to. Things have got to change now that *Daed*'s gone, and I've got a *familie*. This farm will fail if we don't make some changes."

Almeda raised a hand, indicating she'd heard enough. "I'm thinking things through."

"Think harder!" Eli snapped.

"It'll be for the best," Nella echoed.

Florene sat in silence. The argument was hard to listen to. Anxious to escape the Kestlers' drama, she stood. "*Danke* for the lovely meal," she said, scooping up a handful of dishes and cutlery. "Let me help clean up."

Almeda shook her head. "*Nein*. After what you've been through, you need to sit and rest." She waved a hand toward her daughter-in-law. "Nella can do them."

Nella pushed out a heavy sigh. "Of course, I will," she grumbled. "No matter that I've barely had an hour of sleep all week." She didn't have a chance to pick up a dish. Isaiah started wailing at the top of his lungs.

Eli's shoulders slumped. "*Ach*, no, not again. We just got him down."

Crossing into the living room, Nella lifted the fussy *boppli* out of his bassinet. Tiny hands were clenched into fists, and the infant's legs were curled up. Cradling him in the crook of her arm, she patted his belly in a steady rhythm. The soothing motion brought a moment of quiet.

"He's not wet," she said, checking his diaper.

"Could be he's hungry again," Almeda suggested. "See if he will take a bottle."

"I'll warm his formula," Eli volunteered, pushing his empty plate away. "I'd like to listen to my afternoon ball game in peace."

"I'll be glad when his colic passes and he sleeps more," Nella said.

Measuring the formula into a bottle, Eli popped it into a battery-powered warmer.

"I never knew one *boppli* would be so troublesome."

Almeda looked between the two young parents. "You've both got a lot to learn. Isaiah's just getting started and soon there'll be more underfoot."

Nella rolled her eyes. The notion didn't appear to appeal to her, at all. "We might wait awhile before we try for another." She glanced toward her busy *ehmann*. Occupied with his task at the counter, Eli had turned his back toward the womenfolk. "A *long* while," she mouthed to keep her words from his ears.

Florene carried the dishes to the sink. "I can clean up," she said. "It'll help keep my hands busy." As she ran water into the basin, a pang of uncertainty attacked. The room seemed to shrink around her, enveloping her in the responsibilities that awaited. The weight of impending mother-hood pressed against her. She wondered if she possessed the patience and fortitude required to care for a little one.

"I don't know what's wrong with this child," Nella complained. "Maybe we should take him to the doctor."

Bottle in hand, Eli frowned fiercely. "There's nothing wrong with Isaiah!" The couple exchanged helpless glances, their frustration growing.

"There's no getting to town today, anyway," Almeda reminded. "What Isaiah needs is a warm bath and a spoonful of chamomile tea. It's a remedy I used on Eli when he was suffering." Rising from the table, the old woman reached for her cane. She winced with each subtle movement, nursing the injury that had rendered her mobility a challenge.

Eli raised an eyebrow, curiosity replacing frustration. "Chamomile tea? But isn't that for adults?"

Almeda shook her head. "It's amazing what the Lord provides to heal us. Chamomile has a calming effect, even on the tiniest ones. And mind you, don't forget the power of a *mutter*'s touch. After you bathe him, swaddle Isaiah close and let him feel your warmth."

Nella offered a grateful look. "I'll do that." Looking toward her *ehmann*, she added, "Eli, will you fill his tub?"

"*Ja*, I will." Eli hurried to the task, anxious to soothe his frazzled *ehefrau* and fussy *boppli*. Babe in arms, Nella trailed him to the washroom at the end of a short hall.

Almeda limped toward the cupboard. Taking down a tin canister, she carefully measured fragrant, dried chamomile flowers into a thick stoneware mug.

Filling the kettle to the brim, Florene set it on the stovetop. "I'll heat some water."

"*Danke.*"

"I'm happy to help." Returning to the table, she finished clearing away the dirty dishes. "Just tell me what needs to be done. I'll earn my place."

Almeda's stoic expression broke into a faint smile. The lines on her stern face softened. "You're welcome to stay as long as you like. If I were to say it out loud, it's been a struggle to keep things in order since Eli married Nella."

"Oh?" Almeda's comment begged for an explanation. But rather than pry, Florene began washing the dishes. Giving each a thorough wipe with a rag, she stacked them in a metal rack to dry. Her silence was an invitation that her ears were open, and she was willing to listen.

"I don't think Nella's happy here," the older woman suddenly blurted. "Getting hitched, moving away from all she's known, and then having a *youngie* right away. A lot of changes for a woman to go through."

Florene nodded. "I'd agree."

Almeda pursed her lips. "And country living's not for everyone, especially for someone used to living in town. I'm afraid Nella is missing her friends and *familie*. We only get to town once a week—for church and supplies. In the summer, that might be enough socializing. But in the winter—" She glanced toward the window. Past the protective layer of glass, the elements howled. "We're on our own if the weather goes bad."

Florene wiped her damp hands with a towel. "I understand. I often wished we lived in town where the fun things were." It was true. Spending days tending the livestock on her *familie* ranch had felt boring and old-fashioned to her.

"Nella's *daed* spoiled her," Almeda continued. "She grew up in a fine *haus*. Out here, we've always been on the poor side. Our place is old and we've lived the same way for a coon's age."

Florene smiled, thinking of her sister and brother-in-law. "Gail still fights with her old wood-burning stove. Levi says they'll update, but I doubt they ever will. That old thing's been in our *familie* for generations and she won't part with it." As she spoke, another pang of homesickness washed through her. Trying not to let her emotions show, she blinked back the moisture rimming her eyes. She wanted to go home. Desperately.

Almeda's gaze brushed her face. "I'm glad you've come," she said softly. "I believe *Gott* knew you needed a place. An extra set of hands is a blessing right now. And I can't help but think you might be the *freundin* Nella needs."

"Of course." Though many years had parted them, she genuinely hoped she could reconnect with her old school chum. Having stayed in the Amish community, Nella could help guide and advise her as she eased back into Plain living. It would be *gut* to rekindle old friendships. A small step, but one she hoped was the first of many.

The kettle whistled, breaking into the conversation.

"Better get this tea made," Almeda said, carrying it to the counter.

Dishes done, Florene looked over the leftovers. A lot of food had been prepared—most of it meant to feed the mountain that was Gilead Kestler.

"Gil didn't come to eat." She glanced out a nearby window. A small cabin stood in the distance, catty-corner from the barn. A gently sloping roof adorned with hand-forged metalwork protected the structure against the elements. Crafted with skill, the structure bore the hallmark of a bygone era, a testament to a simpler way of life.

That must be his place.

"Didn't have much for breakfast, either." Worry crossed Almeda's face. "He's most likely starved, but he's too stubborn to come back."

"I don't know if I would come back, either. Eli was kind of mean."

"Eli was just teasing," Almeda said, attempting to explain away her younger *sohn*'s bad behavior. "Gil's used to it. He'll get over it and they'll be fine."

Florene wasn't convinced it was true. The hurt shadowing Gil's expression was heartbreaking. Eli's barbed words had stung hard, visibly grinding the big man's feelings into dust. It was her fault the matter had even come up. Opening a Bible after so many years of ignoring *Gott*'s word had scared her. She wasn't a believer anymore. Nor was she confident she ever would be again. A strange emptiness gripped her soul, a cold, hollow void yet to be filled. "Why don't I make some sandwiches and bring them over?"

"Would you mind? I'm sure he'd like to have it." Almeda pointed to a space under the cabinet. "There's a wicker basket you can use. And you can borrow my coat, too. It's on the peg by the door."

"*Danke.* That will be perfect." She put generous slices of wood-smoked ham between extra-thick slices of bread. A thick wedge of sharp cheddar accompanied the last slice of apple pie. Wrapping the meal in cheesecloth, she filled the basket.

It's the least I can do, she thought.

She owed Gil Kestler a debt of gratitude.

She intended to pay it back.

A man needed to know how to look out for himself before he could take care of a *fraa* and *kinder.*

That was what *Daed* had always said.

Gil had lately come to believe it meant something else. He'd have to take care of himself because no one else would.

The fire in the cookstove had burnt down to embers. Feeling the chill hovering around the edges of the room, he knelt in front of the stove. He swept the ash into a metal pail and selected a few logs from the neatly stacked pile in the corner. The knotted veins of the wood promised a slow, steady burn that would warm the long afternoon ahead. Adding kindling and pieces of paper, he struck a match. Flames quickly devoured the wood.

Declining to return to the farmhouse, he'd decided to prepare his own meal. The barbs Eli flung at him still stung. Distancing himself in solitude would give him time to think. And pray.

A pang of loneliness coursed through him, but pride held firm. After Eli got married, the boundaries of kinship were subtly redrawn. Slowly, but surely, he was being edged to the side in favor of his *bruder*'s new *familie*.

Feeling isolation seep into his bones, he sighed. It wasn't that he begrudged Eli his happiness. However, the shift in dynamics left him feeling lonelier than ever. Envy clawed, digging deeper.

His gaze settled on his grandfather's Bible. A treasured heirloom, the book sat by the old man's favorite rocking chair. He often sat in that same chair, searching the frayed pages, praying *Gott* would give him the ability to decipher the precious words.

"Wrath killeth the foolish man, and envy slayeth the silly one," he murmured, reciting one of the many passages he'd memorized. Seeking comfort in the sacred verses calmed him. He hadn't meant to think badly about Eli.

A minute ticked away in silence. Another followed. The iron stove crackled softly, radiating a gentle heat throughout the cabin. The home he'd made for himself was just fine for a single fellow.

Gott provided what a man was supposed to have when he was supposed to have it. He had everything he needed. The simple wooden table covered by a blue-and-white checkered cloth gave him a place to eat his meals. A modest bed adorned with handmade quilts gave him a place to lay his head. Well-worn chairs and other odd pieces of furniture offered a comfortable place to sit and rest after a hard day's work. There was no indoor bathroom, but he did have running water. A hand-pumped spigot over a tin washtub served up a steady stream from the nearby well house. The simplicity of the furniture, the absence of modern appliances and the glow of the kerosene lamp created an atmosphere of serene humility. It wasn't anything fancy like some of the houses other Amish folks living in town had. But it was shelter, and he was grateful for the roof over his head.

A knock shattered his solitude.

Gil rose, brushing ashes off his clothes. He wasn't expecting anyone, but the fact someone had come was welcome. *Maybe it's Eli, coming to say he's sorry.* That would be nice. He'd be willing to accept an apology. He always did.

Unlatching the door, he pulled it open. A woman stood outside, bundled in a colorful patchwork coat. Recycled out of old quilts, the coat belonged to *Mamm.* But his mother wasn't the one wearing it.

"Florene, what are you doing out here?"

Head dipping back, his visitor offered a smile. "You didn't come back for lunch." She held out a wicker basket. "I brought you a few things to eat."

"Danke," he said, accepting her offering. "I appreciate the kindness."

But she didn't leave. She lingered. The snow flurried around her slender figure, dusting her with white flakes. "Aren't you going to invite me in?"

Gil shifted his weight from foot to foot. *Nay.* He wasn't. It was against the norms, the unspoken rules that governed the behaviors of Plain folks. The clash between the desire to be a *gut* host and the adherence to tradition created a palpable tension.

"It's not proper."

Amusement crinkled the edges of her eyes. "I think it's okay. We're not courting, and I'm not Amish. The rules are different for us, don't you think?"

"I guess it would be all right." He wasn't a baptized member of the church. Until he made a permanent commitment, he was free to do as he wished.

Stepping inside, Florene brushed off the snowflakes. "I promise not to stay long." She looked around, taking in the interior. "I remember visiting my grandparents' cabin when I was little. It's like stepping back in time, but in the best way." Her curious gaze swept toward the table set with dishes and utensils. "Did you already have something?"

"*Nay.* I was just about to bake up some corn pone." A simple but hearty dish, the dense bread was easy to mix and quick to bake.

"My *mamm* used to make that for us all the time when I was little."

"I like it with buttermilk," he said, placing the basket on the table.

Florene brightened. "Me, too." Nervously, she clasped her hands in front of her body. "I'll be glad to set everything out for you. Like a *fraa* should."

A sigh slipped past his lips. "Never had one."

"Well, pretend. Just for fun." Shrugging out of her coat, she hung it on a peg beside his and then brushed the wrinkles out of her apron. "Now I look like a proper wife."

"*Ja*. You do."

Fluttering around, Florene unpacked the basket. "Your *mamm* wouldn't let Eli have the last piece of pie," she said, explaining as she unwrapped the dishes. "She said it wasn't fair for him to have most of it to himself."

Gil laughed. "I bet he didn't like that."

"He didn't." She waved her hands. "Eat. It won't keep all day."

Gil sat. Careful not to put his elbows on the table, he pressed his palms together and bowed his head. The Lord had provided generously and abundantly.

His stomach rumbled, reminding him he needed a meal. *"Danke, Gott, für dieses essen,"* he said, hurrying through the blessing.

"Amen," Florene added. She obviously respected his need to offer thanks, and the discomfort she'd displayed during Bible study wasn't as readily apparent.

He scooped up a sandwich. The scent of fresh bread embracing the thick slices of applewood ham sent out an enticing aroma. He took a bite, savoring the rich, smoky flavor. It tasted wonderful. He tried not to wolf it down in a few bites.

Florene glanced toward the cookstove. "Would you mind if I made some tea?"

"I could stand a cup." He nodded toward the little cupboard near the cookstove. "It's just there."

Nodding, she set to the task. She set the kettle on the stove and rummaged around before pulling out a small tin. Scooping out a few tablespoons of dried herbs, she added them to the water. The fragrant blend of chamomile, peppermint and lemon balm scented the air. She strained the golden liquid into two cups and delivered the steaming brew to the table.

"I'd forgotten the taste of homemade tea." Taking a sip, she briefly closed her eyes to enjoy the flavor. "Store-bought is so bland compared to this."

"*Mammi* enjoyed making her own," he said, speaking of his grandmother. "She believed you shouldn't spend money on anything the good Lord provided from the garden. *Mamm*'s like that, too."

"My *mamm* did the same thing," she said. "And

my sisters won't buy what they can make or grow themselves."

"When the weather clears, you should go and see them," he urged. "Let them know you're safe."

Florene shook her head. "Life took us on different paths. I never thought I'd find myself back here. But I don't know if I could go back home after what I—" She suddenly cut herself short. The shadows haunting her gaze spoke volumes. Her shoulders visibly carried the weight of regret.

Gil nodded, respecting her privacy. He couldn't begin to fathom the pain she must feel, being apart from her kin. The bonds of *familie* were the threads that wove their people together. It pained him to see her so alone.

I'll do my best to help, he decided. The Lord would expect no less.

He continued to eat with the contented peacefulness that came with the enjoyment of a warm hearth, *gut* food and pleasant company. The rhythmic clink of his utensils against the stoneware echoed in the stillness. Between bites, he stole a few glances at his visitor. The simplicity of the moment was not lost on him; it was a feast not only for the body but for the spirit. He was glad he'd asked her in. Nothing improper about it. Just two folks enjoying a visit.

Captivated by her grace, he couldn't fail to notice how the flickering lamplight played on her features. The illumination cast a soft glow that seemed to accentuate her beauty. Touched by her presence, his mind wandered into the realm of what-ifs. What if Florene could be more than just a *freundin*?

It was a silly notion, of course. One he dare not speak aloud. Still, his heart silently wrestled with loneliness and the desire for companionship.

Florene finished her tea and put her empty cup aside. Brushing her lips with a napkin, she thoughtfully pressed it into neat folds. "I didn't get a chance to apologize. I'm sorry for what I did."

Gil blinked, clueless. "Sorry for what?" She'd done nothing wrong.

"When I tried to give you the Bible. I didn't know you couldn't—um—read."

"*Ja*, it's true. I can't. I never learned." Embarrassed, he looked away.

"It's no big deal," Florene said, her voice filled with understanding. "I can show you how…if you'll let me." Laughing, she added, "Rebecca was a schoolmarm, you know, so it sort of runs in the *familie*."

Surprise took him aback. "Do you think I could?" He'd gotten pulled out of school so young that he barely recalled going.

"I don't know why not. We'll work on it, together." Compassion flickering in her gaze, she added, "What do you say?"

Touched by her sincerity, Gil felt joy spreading

through his chest. He had carried the weight of illiteracy like a burden, a silent struggle concealed behind a stoic facade. For someone to acknowledge it, to offer a helping hand, was an unexpected balm to his wounded pride.

Hope mingled with gratitude. Her offer was a true gift. One he would willingly accept.

"Ja," he nodded eagerly. "Please, teach me."

Chapter Five

Gil woke from sleep with a sense of anticipation he hadn't felt in years. The chill filling the cabin nipped at his nose as he abandoned the cocoon of his warm bed. His breath hung in the frigid air, a visible reminder of winter's grip. His bare feet met the cold wooden floor, and he winced.

Hurrying to dress, he slipped on his shirt and trousers. A pair of heavy woolen socks and his sturdy work boots followed. "I could do without this weather, Lord," he muttered.

Shivering a little, he headed toward the stove. Last night's fire had burned down to ashes. Stirring the embers, he added fresh wood and kindling. Hearty flames roared back to life. The old stove crackled and hissed, as if expressing gratitude for the attention. Heating water in a large pot, he poured it into a basin for bathing.

Giving himself a quick wash, he bundled into his heavy coat. Then he plunked his hat on his head and headed out for breakfast. The sun was just beginning to peer over the far horizon, painting the frigid landscape with a gentle glow. The crisp snow shimmered like white silk. The storm had transformed the world. But it was far from over. Blustering wind and leaden clouds threatened to throw down more of the icy mix. The air was brisk, carrying the scent of frost.

His journey to the farmhouse wasn't long, but every step seemed slower than the last as he trudged through the deep snow. Eli's request hovered in the back of his mind. Giving his brother more land would mean he'd have to cut back the horses. To keep the animals fed, but not overgraze the land, each animal required a minimum of two to four acres. He could cull the Mustangs, keeping the stronger ones and selling off the rest.

Doable. But did he want to?

No. He didn't. The land was his legacy, one he should rightfully inherit, as his *vater* promised. Surely *Mamm* wouldn't give in to Eli's demands. If she did, it would snatch his future—his living—out from under his feet. But the final say wasn't his. All he could do was pray *Gott* would give *Mamm* the wisdom she needed to make the right decision.

A sigh slipped past his lips. Later, he'd pray on the matter, too. There had to be a solution that would suit all concerned. For now, he had a lot to do, and time was slipping away. Problems and chores weren't the only thing tumbling through his mind. Florene had promised to teach him to read.

Smiling, he glanced toward the sky and grinned. "I can't wait to learn more of your words, Lord." Soon he hoped he would be able to unravel the mystery of books.

The back door opened before he reached his destination. "I wondered if I'd see your face today," *Mamm* called, gesturing for him to hurry up. "I hope you're hungry. The food's almost done."

Gil stepped up on the porch, stomping his feet. "I'm over being mad at Eli."

Mamm stepped back, allowing him inside. "Glad to hear it."

"What's said is said." Pushing the door shut, Gil hung up his hat before shrugging out of his coat.

Leaning on her cane, *Mamm* looked him up and down. "Don't you have any clean clothes?"

Gil glanced down. His shirt and trousers were stained and wrinkled from yesterday's work. He'd thought little about it when he'd put them on. Why put on clean clothes when all he'd be doing was mucking out stalls and other chores? Come the end of the day, he'd just be grubby all over again.

He shrugged. "No one cares how I look."

Mamm stiffened. "I care," she said, giving him a swat. "The least you could do is pull back that tangle you call hair and try to look decent. And put your razor across the strop, too."

Gil ran his hand over a stubbled cheek. The

scraggly growth was only scraped off once or twice a month. "I guess I should."

"You're of an age when the chance to get a *fraa* is slipping through your fingers."

"Don't know that I ever had one."

Mamm shook her head. "You could try a little harder," she commented before hobbling back to her cookstove. "I'll have breakfast on the table shortly."

"Sounds *gut*," he said, glad to change the subject. He'd never cared much about his looks because he didn't think any woman would, either.

Florene came down the stairs. Cradling Isaiah, she moved with care, careful not to jostle the infant. "Nella's not feeling well," she said, speaking in a hushed tone as she joined them in the kitchen. "I thought I would bring him down so she could rest."

Mamm looked up from her cooking. "*Danke* for lending a hand."

Florene shifted the bundle she carried. The infant was nestled snugly, a tiny hand peeking out from under a carefully swaddled blanket. "I don't mind," she said, smiling down at the little one. "He's such a cutie."

Gil silently agreed. His gaze lingered on her, captivated by the tender care she gave his nephew. A quiet yearning stirred within him.

"Morning, Florene."

Her gaze momentarily locked with his. "Morning, Gilead," she said softly, speaking his full name. "I hope you slept well last night."

Flustered, he averted his gaze. Normally a sure-footed man, he suddenly felt like a stumbling colt.

Isaiah began to fuss, making a mewling sound. "Gaaaa-uh."

"I think that means he's hungry." Attention diverted, Florene glanced toward the counter where the *boppli*'s formula and bottle warmer sat. Without warning, she stepped toward Gil, offering him the infant. "Would you hold him for a minute?"

He panicked, moving out of reach. "I've never held him. Nella's afraid I'll hurt him." When *Mamm* wasn't around, his sister-in-law sneered at him, calling him an ugly brute.

Florene persisted. "Oh, she's being silly. Babies are sturdier than you think. Just cradle him in your arms."

"Help the girl out," *Mamm* urged.

Gil kept his distance. "I don't want to get in trouble."

"Don't be silly," Florene said, stepping in front of him. "Here, do it just like this." She demonstrated, guiding his hands and arms to support the *boppli*'s head and body in the correct position. "Gently. Not too tight."

As the warmth of the infant seeped in, Gil couldn't help but marvel at the delicate wonder in his grasp. The joy of holding his precious little nephew filled him. He cradled the tiny bundle, marveling at the innocence in Isaiah's bright eyes.

Isaiah cooed, his fussing replaced with contentment. "Blaaa," he burbled.

"See? You're a natural." Hands free, Florene set to her task. Measuring out the formula, she popped the bottle in the warmer. "Be just a minute."

Gil cuddled Isaiah closer. Enchanted, he felt a sense of wonder and delight. A dream flickered in his mind. For a minute, he allowed himself to envision a future where he, too, could share such tender moments with his own *sohn*. His imagination briefly painted a picture of domestic bliss.

Done with the bacon, *Mamm* carried the platter to the table. Leaning on her cane made the task difficult, but she managed. "Don't know why Nella's so fussy," she groused. "You've got *gut* hands. Strong hands."

"That's just the way she is," Gil said, accepting the fact that his sister-in-law would never like him. Still, he refused to let it spoil his delight. His grin widened as he tickled the *boppli* under the chin. The baby's plump fingers grasped onto one of his, creating a connection that felt both fragile and unbreakable.

And then it all shattered.

Eli came down the stairs. Yawning and stretching, he pulled his suspenders over his shoulders. His eyes widened with concern as he observed the sight in the kitchen. "What are you doing with Isaiah?"

Gil's insides knotted. He knew the rule and had broken it. "Just helping out."

Eli's expression tightened. "You know how Nella feels." Striding over, he plucked the infant away. "You said you'd take care of him," he added, throwing a dismissive glance toward Florene. "That didn't mean handing him over to Gil."

"I don't see a problem," she said in her defense. "A woman's only got two hands. Gil was holding Isaiah while I got his bottle ready."

"Gil wasn't doing any harm," *Mamm* added, stepping into the fray. She eyed Eli from head to foot. "If you were so worried about your *sohn*, maybe you should have been tending him yourself."

Eli's gaze softened, but his frown remained. "You know how Nella and Gil don't get along."

Gil's heart sank. He didn't think he'd done anything wrong, but it was better to keep the peace. "I'm sorry. I didn't mean to make any trouble."

Eli sighed. "I wouldn't say anything myself. But Nella's his mother and she has a right to her feelings."

Gil nodded, his gaze briefly dropping to the floor. "I understand."

Mamm gave her head a shake. "Always one thing or another with that girl," she muttered.

"Everyone does their best to help, but it's never enough."

As if picking up on his father's anxiety, Isaiah began to fuss. A cry burbled up from deep in his tiny chest. Tension filled the kitchen, the air heavy with unspoken emotions. Isaiah's piercing cries filled the air.

"I didn't mean to snap." Eli rocked the infant, attempting to quiet him. "Come on, Isaiah. Don't cry. Please."

Mamm shook her head over the entire sorry matter. "What's the matter with Nella?"

"She's feeling nauseous," Eli explained. "I came down to get her a cup of tea and some toast."

The old woman pursed her lips. "*Ach*, hope it isn't that virus. Not a *gut* time for anyone to get sick."

"The flu is going around," Eli continued. "Always does when folks are cooped up indoors."

"That, or she's expecting another *boppli*," *Mamm* said.

Eli paled. "Surely not so soon."

Out of the corner of his eye, Gil caught a glimpse of Florene. Pressing a hand against her stomach, she glanced down at her slender middle. As she raised her head, there was a brief, almost imperceptible, tightening of her lips that betrayed an emotion she seemed determined to conceal. She looked vulnerable, lost.

Something's on her mind, he thought, tucking

the moment away. He didn't know what it meant, but her silent gesture touched him.

Mouth puckering, *Mamm* pushed out a sigh. "I'll make a tray. Some elderberry tea will calm Nella's ills."

Eli's gaze swept toward a nearby window. "Don't think I'm up to going out today, either," he said, coughing lightly. "I'm feeling a little feverish, too."

Gil turned away, attempting to hide his dismay by taking a seat at the table. Yep. He should have seen it coming. The responsibilities that should be shared between them usually came to rest solely on his shoulders. His *bruder* always found an excuse when he didn't feel like working.

No reason to argue, he thought. *I'll get things done faster without him.*

But not before he had a proper breakfast to fuel his efforts. Snagging a piece of bacon from the plate *Mamm* had set on the table, he pushed it into his mouth. "I can handle things fine."

"I'll help, too," a shy voice added.

Surprised, Gil glanced toward Florene. He'd enjoyed her company yesterday and wouldn't care if she tagged along. "You don't mind? It's awfully cold out."

"Not at all." Anticipation brightened her gaze. A warm smile played on her lips. "I saw you kept rabbits. I'd love to see them."

* * *

The barn looked a lot different in the dim morning illumination.

Florene stopped and took in her surroundings—a collection of tools, bales of hay and stalls filled with animals rustling fitfully in their confined spaces. Her breath caught in the musty scents, and her mind rewound to her harrowing arrival. Time folded, transporting her back to the heart of the tempest. The relentless assault of snow, the biting cold that seeped through every layer of clothing—all were etched vividly in her mind.

Just when it seemed she could take no more, the dim structure had appeared. A beacon of hope amid chaos, it was her saving grace. The massive space had been pitch-black when she stumbled inside. Pushing the creaking doors shut behind her, she'd collapsed on a mound of straw. With the howling winds muffled, a comforting warmth had enveloped her. The storm raged outside, but within the secure walls, she'd found a haven.

Closing her eyes, she inhaled deeply to calm her nervous pulse. *I lived.*

"Are you okay?" Gil asked.

Shivering, Florene managed a nod. "I didn't think I'd make it," she admitted, voice trembling. "I don't know what I would have done if—"

"You're safe now. *Gott* knew where to guide you."

Glancing away, Florene pursed her lips. Was the Lord truly watching over her? Or was it just a series of fortunate events? As much as she wanted to believe, she was still having trouble reconciling with the benevolent deity she'd once worshiped in church. Had *Gott* heard her pleas? She wasn't sure. It often felt like her prayers were swallowed by an indifferent void.

Blinking hard, she forced a smile. "Can I see the rabbits?" It was easier to change the subject than address her complicated emotions. She wasn't ready to deal with them. Not yet.

Maybe not ever, her mind added.

Gil nodded. *"Ja."* He led her to a multilevel pen in a corner of the barn. Constructed with functionality in mind, it had a latched door opening into an outdoor enclosure. It was securely fenced, meant to protect the hares from predators while allowing them to indulge in natural behaviors. Unlatching the wire gate, he invited her to step inside. A flurry of fluffy tails scattered.

Happy for the distraction, Florene dropped to her knees in front of the hutches. The rabbits, normally a lively bunch, were huddled together, their twitching noses and wide eyes revealing their unease.

Dipping into the wicker basket she carried, she pulled out a handful of vegetables. Almeda had let her have scraps, including diced carrots, potatoes, celery and rutabaga. She scattered the leavings as an enticement. Abandoning their wariness, the animals gave in to their curiosity. One by one, they hopped out to investigate. Soon they were nibbling the treats with gusto.

Florene gently scooped up a ruby-eyed rabbit with a black splotch on its nose.

"Oh, he's adorable." As she cradled the large buck, her heart swelled with a mix of nostalgia and yearning.

Leaning against the sturdy rail, Gil nudged the edge of his hat away from his eyes. "Reminds me of when you were little. I remember you had a goat and it followed you around like a dog."

Florene laughed. "Her name was Sassy," she said, surprised he'd noticed her back then. A couple of times a year, he would show up at the ranch with a trailer, unloading the horses her *daed* had purchased from him. Back in those days, she was both intrigued and intimidated by his brawny figure. He dwarfed most average-sized men. Watching him handle the mustangs, she'd often wondered what it felt like to have the power to tame the wild animals.

Amusement crinkled the edges of his eyes. "It sure was cute. Always wondered how you got that goat so tame."

"Sassy was a foundling," she explained, picturing a tiny bundle of fur with legs that seemed too big for its body. "Kicked aside by the others after she was born." Favorite memories flashed through her mind. Sassy often managed to escape her pen, only to be found nibbling in the vegetable garden or perched on the porch steps, proud of her small rebellions. The little goat would often nuzzle her hand, a silent expression of the unspoken bond they shared. Sassy had later passed away at a ripe old age.

"Kind of know how that feels." The normally confident set of his jaw quivered ever so slightly, betraying the internal turmoil churning inside.

Compassion flowed through her, mingling with the facts as she knew them. "I know better," she blurted before thinking twice. "I saw how you handled Isaiah. You were gentle as could be."

"I wouldn't hurt him." Sorrow shadowed the big man's expression. "But Nella—she's always on me."

"I don't see why." Florene had witnessed with her own eyes how his sister-in-law's disapproval kept Gil confined to the fringes of the *familie*. He wasn't a danger, but that's how Nella treated him.

"'Cause I—" He suddenly pursed his lips, silencing himself. An emotional storm raged beneath the surface of his calm.

"What?"

"Well, nothing," he finished in a mumble. "That's just the way Nella is. Eli, too. He eggs her on." A long sigh of frustration punctuated his words.

Puzzled by his hesitation, Florene let the rabbit go. Climbing to her feet, she brushed away the hay clinging to her legs. She couldn't begin to guess what Gil had meant to say. But from what she'd observed, he'd always been treated as an outsider. He wasn't comely. He wasn't smart. He was a square peg trying to fit into a round hole.

Kind of like me. Born and raised Amish, she'd always felt like a traveler in a strange land. Saddled by the restrictions of the *Ordnung*, she'd done her best to buck the yoke of tradition.

"I see how they treat you." Her gaze searched his for a connection. "It's not right."

Gil's lips curled into a faint, appreciative smile. "*Ja*, it hurts. More than I can say." He kicked at the hay beneath his worn leather boots, the weight on his spirit unbudging. "But I love my *familie*, and I want to do what's best for them."

"I believe that," she said softly.

"I pray all the time *Gott* will show Nella I mean no harm. And that Eli will stop picking on me so bad."

Her gaze homed in, pinning him down. "Do you believe the Lord hears us?"

He nodded. "*Ja*. I do." His reply carried the weight of absolute conviction.

"What if He doesn't? What if there are no answers?"

Gil paused, eyes squinting at the corners as he searched for the right words. "*Not now* is an answer, too. Some things are meant to come later. When we're ready. Sometimes we ask too soon."

"And if *Gott* says no?" she pressed.

A shrug rolled off the big man's shoulders. "I accept it and move on. That's what I do. No reason to be angry or upset. That's why I don't stay mad at Eli and Nella. *Gott* will deal with them in His own time. Just like he does everyone. Staying mad doesn't do me any *gut*. Carrying anger poisons a man inside. I don't want anger in me, so I pray it away."

Florene searched Gil's face. His expression held a depth that spoke of a profound connection to his beliefs. His voice held a quiet strength, resonating with the certainty that his faith had been tested and proven. His words were humble. Respectful.

Unbidden tears blurred her vision. *I wish I could have that.*

The peaceful exchange was suddenly disrupted by a chorus of restless animal noises. The barn seemed to come alive with the lively commotion of cows lowing, chickens clucking and horses stomping their hooves impatiently in their stalls. The source of this uproar became apparent as a mischievous pair of barn cats chased each other.

Snatching up one of the cats as it ran by, Gil gave the squirming feline a calming stroke. "Plume, you're getting too riled up."

Games interrupted, the large tomcat yowled.

Gil set the animal free. The cat darted back toward its companion and the chase. "You're better off catching mice rather than playing games," he warned with a laugh. Sobering, he added, "Guess I'd best stop flapping my jaws and get some work done."

"What can I do?" Florene asked, tucking away their heartfelt conversation. Later, when she was alone, she had a lot of thinking to do.

"It'd be a big help if you'd throw out some scratch for the chickens and gather the eggs." He reached for a bucket, dipping it into a barrel. "I'll tend the horses and cows."

Happy to keep her hands busy, Florene set to her task. The hens clucked softly as she scattered a mixture of grains for a treat. She also refilled their troughs with fresh water. As the chickens pecked up their meal, she reached into the nests, collecting the freshly laid eggs. Counting more than a dozen, she tucked them into her basket.

Nostalgia tugged, and she couldn't help but yearn for the idyllic days of her childhood. She imagined her unborn *boppli* surrounded by the same love and simplicity that had shaped her upbringing. But her path back to the Amish community was still uncertain. Her connection to the church had unraveled years ago.

She frowned as her pleasant thoughts evaporated. Doubt grew stronger, deftly strangling hope with vicious precision. Despair settled over her like a heavy shroud. She felt isolated and alone, torn between two worlds that seemed irreconcilable.

How could she find her way back when she was the one who'd walked away?

Chapter Six

The soft glow of the kerosene lamp flickered through the cozy room as Florene cradled Isaiah in her arms. The infant rested easily, blissfully snuggled in his blanket. Gazing down on his face, she marveled at his tiny features—the delicate nose, rosebud lips and tiny tufts of light brown hair peeking out. He was perfect.

"*Ach*, you're a precious one," she murmured.

Pressing the heel of her boot against the floor, she kept the chair rocking in a steady rhythm. Her breathing was soft, which in turn soothed the *boppli*. The cracking glow of a fire in the nearby hearth chased away the chill lingering in the air.

Content to sit, she let her mind drift back to an earlier hour. After helping Gil tend the livestock, she'd returned to chaos. The old farmhouse was in an uproar. Nerves stretched tight, Nella had collapsed. Bursting into tears as she attempted to care for her bawling infant, she'd retreated upstairs. An argument with Eli hadn't helped. Flustered by his wife's frustrations—not to mention the close quarters they were all shoved into—he'd stomped outside to simmer in his discontent. Almeda did her best to mediate, but wasn't successful. Gil wisely steered clear, preferring to tend his horses.

Snared in the tension, Florene had rolled up her sleeves and stepped in. She didn't know why Nella and Eli were snapping at each other, but it didn't matter. Someone needed her for a change, and not the other way around. Lending a hand was not just a task; it was a way for her to express her gratitude, to repay the kindness bestowed upon her.

Settling the old woman in a comfortable chair with a cup of tea, she'd tucked Nella into bed. Isaiah needed the most attention. Tiny face flushed, he'd let out a series of cries punctuated by little gasps. Colic had its hold on him, making him difficult to handle.

Florene had scooped him out of his bassinet, and discovered a wonderful thing she hadn't known before. The tasks of changing diapers, warming bottles and walking the floor became not burdens, but joy. She marveled at the vulnerability and innocence of the *boppli*, finding contentment in the simplicity of caring for a little soul so utterly dependent. Her nurturing touch worked. Isaiah had finally settled down, succumbing to sleep.

All was calm. Peaceful. The tension gripping the old house had receded.

Adjusting Isaiah's covers, she softly hummed an old Amish lullaby. The melody's gentle words of comfort were cherished, repeated through generations. As she sang, she couldn't help but think about her own pending motherhood.

Emotion tightened her throat. The weight of responsibility threatened to crush her. She had no means to raise the child.

I'm not ready.

A fresh rush of tears blurred her vision. She sniffed, blinking hard. The road ahead was uncertain. But she would do her best to navigate it with honesty and courage.

"You're *gut* with little ones," Nella whispered from across the room. "He's so quiet when you hold him."

Florene glanced toward the child's mother. Dressed in a long gown and robe, Nella rested comfortably. She was pale and wan, exhaustion etched around the corners of her eyes and mouth.

As Florene adjusted the blanket around Isaiah, tenderness touched her heart. "I enjoy taking care of him."

Nella giggled with amusement. "Never thought I'd hear you saying those words. When we were in school, I recall you declaring you weren't ever having *youngies.*"

"*Ja.* I suppose I did." Back then, she couldn't fathom why Amish girls were eager to become wives and mothers. She had dreamt of a different life—one filled with adventure and independence. "I'd like to think I've grown up since then. I know I've changed my mind about a lot of things."

"I wish you had been here to change my mind about marrying Eli," Nella groused.

"Oh?"

"I thought living on a farm would be fun, but it's not." Nella cast her gaze around with a tinge of disdain. "Now I'm stuck out here in this dump, all by myself."

"That's not true. Almeda's here to help."

"*Ach*, that old busybody." Shifting with discontent, Nella rolled her eyes. "She's no help, lame foot or not." Simmering with disappointment, she seemed determined to complain about everything that annoyed her.

"Gil's willing to lend a hand."

Nella stiffened. "He's not allowed to hold Isaiah!" she snapped. "He's too big and can't be trusted."

"Don't be silly. He does fine with the *boppli*."

"Gil's not as nice as everyone thinks he is."

"Oh?"

Nella nodded emphatically. "Eli told me there's darkness in Gil's past, back when he was in school. He was big, even then, and—" The bedridden woman hesitated, her gaze shifting to the fire. "Almeda won't talk about it, but that man has a bad temper."

That said, a heavy silence settled between the two women. The room felt smaller, confined, the walls closing in on all sides.

Florene cradled Isaiah closer, her gaze flickering between the innocent face of the baby and the troubled expression on his *mutter*'s face. She understood the weight of past mistakes, having made her own when she'd abandoned the community. But the Amish were also forgiving folks and believed in second chances. Surely no one would condemn a young *boi* for…*what*?

Questions spun through her mind. What had Gil done that was so terrible?

She sighed. "I honestly don't know what to think."

Nella looked torn, emotions playing across her face. "It happened a long time ago."

A light tap on the door interrupted.

Eli poked his head in. "I'm just checking to make sure Isaiah's okay." Face etched with lines of concern, he stood hesitantly at the threshold.

Nella looked up, her weary gaze holding a flicker of hurt. "He's fine," she said, flagging a hand toward the rocking chair. "Florene finally got him to sleep."

Eli nodded. "That's *gut*. You both need to rest." Stepping into the room, he tiptoed over to check his *sohn*. The worn wooden floor creaked beneath his boots.

Feeling the infant stir, Florene made a shushing sound. "He's fine," she mouthed.

Nella gave her *ehmann* a cross look. "I'm fine, too," she grumbled. "Not that you care."

Stepping away, Eli knelt at her bedside. *"Es tut mir leid,"* he said softly, his apology carrying the weight of remorse. "My words were harsh. I should have never spoken to you in anger."

"All I asked was how much longer?" Unable to contain the storm brewing within her, Nella's voice rose. "We can't keep going on like this. You promised you'd get the—"

Eli cut her short. "Shush!" To silence her, he gave her arm a squeeze. "We'll discuss it later."

Aware her presence had become an intrusion, Florene rose. "I should go," she said, attempting not to jostle Isaiah's peaceful slumber.

Nella held out her arms. "I'll take him."

Florene hesitated. Every time Nella held the child, he bawled incessantly. By now she'd figured out why Isaiah was unsettled and fussy. Nella's stress and anxiety spilled over onto her infant, making them both miserable.

"I don't mind keeping him," she said, unwilling to let him go.

"You need a break," Nella insisted.

No, she didn't. But she had no reason to refuse a mother's request.

"Of course." Florene bent, laying the babe in

his *mutter*'s arms. Thankfully, Isaiah didn't stir. "Can I bring you anything?"

Nella shook her head. *"Nein."*

Reaching the exit, Florene turned. "Call if you need me."

A frown creased El's brow. *"Danke.* We're fine." He waved her out with a thin smile.

Stepping into the dim hallway, Florene pulled the door shut. The brief exchange was peculiar, but not unexpected. A man and his wife were expected to keep their private matters just that. Private.

Reluctance to walk away nagged.

Folding her arms across her chest, Florene leaned into the wall. Since becoming reacquainted with Eli Kestler, she'd discovered she didn't like him. Arrogant and manipulative, he treated his *familie* in a manner that could only be described as demeaning.

She cast her gaze toward the closed door. Her thoughts churned as she contemplated the brief snippet she'd overheard. It was not her intention to pry. But she couldn't shake the feeling something nefarious was unfolding within the walls of the farmhouse.

"Don't know why you're wasting your time," Eli chortled, smirking across the table. "You're slow as molasses."

Frustration simmering, Gil gritted his teeth as

the weight of inadequacy settled in. The worn-out primer he worked from seemed to mock him. Sounding out each letter, he labored to copy simple words onto a slate board. Some words he knew, but others posed a formidable obstacle. Progress was excruciatingly slow. Anything beyond a first-grade level posed a challenge. And it didn't help that Eli wouldn't let up with his teasing.

It would do no *gut* to say something ugly back. Anger wasn't the way to handle his emotions. The Lord warned only a fool uttereth his mind, giving voice to hurtful words. Eli often spoke without caring how he might wound others. But that was the way he'd always been. Everyone accepted it to keep the peace.

"I didn't know learning would be so hard." Yearning for knowledge, he grappled with the lack of education hobbling him in so many ways.

"That's because you haven't got any brains." Eli tapped his temple with a single finger. "Don't know why you need book learning anyway. All you do is break horses. That doesn't take any hard thinking."

Gil's shoulders slumped. The schoolbooks he worked from had belonged to Eli. Cherished as a fond memory of her youngest *sohn*, *Mamm* had tucked them away. But there was nothing from Gil's childhood. He'd barely gotten through the first grade before being yanked out of school and put to work.

As he sneaked a glance across the table, a sigh winnowed past his lips. Eli sat across from him, working a crossword puzzle. Thirsty for entertainment, Eli subscribed to a dozen newspapers and magazines on agriculture and other subjects he found interesting. An Amish *youngie*'s education might end in the eighth grade, but that didn't mean learning stopped. Plain folks cherished knowledge and considered bookstores and the library a valuable resource. Eli had a library card and used it often. Nella read a lot, too. So did *Mamm*. The *Budget* and *Thrifty Living* were her favorites for clipping recipes and catching up on community news.

Somehow, he'd gotten left behind. No one seemed to care if he could read or not. *Daed* often said it wasn't anything a man like him needed anyway. The only thing he was *gut* at was work. He was often summoned to help when someone needed a strong back.

Discouragement clenched hard. *Maybe Eli's right. Maybe I'm too dumb to learn.*

The kitchen fell silent. It was a moment frozen in time, a crossroads between persistence and surrender.

Mamm thankfully had something to say about the matter. "Eli, enough of your teasing. Everyone has their path. Gil is finding his. Leave him be."

Florene backed her up. "Don't pay him no

mind," she urged, nodding over his progress. "You're doing fine."

Eli glowered but retreated. Scooping up his puzzle book, he crossed into the living room. Dropping onto the worn sofa, he put his feet up on the edge of the table. "You're wasting your time."

"I don't agree," Florene breezed back, refusing to be deterred. Since beginning their lessons, she'd been nothing but kind and encouraging. Devising a simple method, she'd begun to teach him how to sound out letters and apply them to what he saw on the page. It was slow going, but he was eager to learn.

Gil's pulse bumped up a notch. Not just from the challenge of his task but also from the presence of someone who seemed to care about his learning. As the evening unfolded, he couldn't help but steal glances at Florene's profile—the soft curve of her *kapp*-framed face, the way her eyes sparkled with genuine pleasure when he grasped a new concept. A subtle knot formed in his stomach each time their gazes met, a testament to the unspoken feelings churning inside him.

"I'm doing my best." At this point in his life, it was more than just a desire. It was a necessity. Learning to read would help connect him to the world around him and give him the tools he needed to keep from being left behind. It would be a disgrace to let ignorance persist when someone was willing to lend a hand. Breaking free from the constraints that had bound him for so many years would be a true blessing.

"It's only been a couple of days," *Mamm* added. "Give it time."

Eli rolled his eyes. "Time's all we've had lately. I know the snow's going to be good for spring planting, but I sure wish it would go away."

Needles clicking, Nella looked up from her knitting. Snug in his bassinet, little Isaiah slept peacefully. "I'm so tired of being stuck in the *haus*," she sighed. "I'd give anything to go to town and visit." Nerves strained, she'd sniped back and forth with anyone who dared to speak to her. To keep the peace, most everyone was walking on eggshells, trying not to upset her.

"I'm sure the roads will be clear enough to travel in another day or two," Florene said, speaking in a positive tone. "Tomorrow, we should see a sunny day."

"I hope so," Nella said, attempting to unravel the yarn she'd snarled into a mess. "These long dark days are so horrible. I've hated being cooped up in this dreary old *haus*."

"It'll get better," Eli promised. "We'll go to town as soon as we can."

Unwilling to engage, *Mamm* kept her thoughts to herself. However, the tension around her eyes and the press of her lips revealed her unhappiness. No one in the old *haus* was happy lately.

Fueled by isolation, everyone acted as if their nerves were taut. The usually warm and inviting atmosphere of the home was transforming into a suffocating prison.

Whether he liked it or not, things were changing. And they were going to continue to change.

Determined not to get distracted, Gil turned his attention back to his slate board. His handwriting was crooked, the letters clumsily formed. The simple words he'd written stared back at him. He silently mouthed them out with a slow, deliberate cadence.

Florene bent over his shoulder to check his progress. "Read back what you've got there."

Gil stiffened, embarrassed by his lack of progress. "I haven't got very far."

She offered a smile. "That's okay. We're not in any hurry." Her encouragement was a comforting anchor.

He nodded. Now if only Eli would shut his mouth and let him concentrate. Instead of offering a helping hand, his younger *bruder* had done nothing but poke at him.

"The cat is fat," he read, placing a finger under each word.

Florene patted his shoulder. "That's *gut*. Now read the next line."

He painstakingly sounded out syllables. "The pig is big."

"Now read the last line."

He pressed on. "The dog is wet."

Eli snickered behind the pages of his magazine. *"Mein bruder ist dumm,"* he said, imitating a slow manner of speech in *Deitsch.*

Mamm snapped. "Eli!" she warned. "I've had enough."

"All right, all right, I'll stop," Eli muttered. "Whatever."

Gil blew out a breath. He tried to focus on what he'd written, but Eli's persistent jibes were like pebbles in his shoes, each one digging deeper with every word. He was tired of the aggravation. He was tired of being teased. The battle wasn't worth the shame he felt.

I give up. Swiping his palm across the surface, he erased the imperfect chalk letters. He might not be the quickest study, but he'd tried his best.

"I'm done." He stared at the blank slate, feeling defeated. "You just can't teach an old dog new tricks."

The room tightened with tension all over again.

Florene straightened the mess he'd made. Closing the primer, she stacked it atop the slate board. "I think that's enough for today. We'll do some more tomorrow."

Gil stubbornly shook his head. *"Nein.* No more. I'm sticking to the things I know."

"Gilead, don't—" *Mamm* started to say.

Gil brushed off her words. Pushing back his chair, he walked to the back door. Claiming his coat and hat, he strode out into the crisp air with determined steps. The far horizon was a canvas of purple streaked with wisps of gray-white clouds that caught the last fading rays of daylight. Glacial air whispered through the skeletal branches of trees, carrying the promise of another chilling night.

The snow yielded beneath his heavy boots as he made his way to the corral. The gentle nickering of horses welcomed him like old friends. In their presence, he found solace. Horses were his language, and in their eyes, he felt no judgment.

He leaned against the fence, his breath forming small clouds in the chilly air. His favorite horse, a majestic creature named Nina, approached him. Smiling, he held out his hand. The mare nuzzled against his palm, offering silent comfort. The bond between them was unspoken but deeply felt. With eyes reflecting trust, the mare lowered her head, inviting more caresses.

"I forgot to bring an apple," he whispered, stroking the animal's sleek mane.

In the serenity of the moment, a woman's voice broke the silence. "Are you okay?"

Gil didn't turn. "Guess so."

"Care for some company?"

"*Nein*. Just leave me be."

Florene walked up, standing beside him. "It doesn't work that way," she said, standing firm. "Once you start something, you need to finish it."

He kept petting the mare. "Don't want to," he mumbled, refusing to look her way. "I'm too dumb."

She stepped closer. "You're not. Don't pay any mind to what Eli says. You're doing well. Better than I thought you could."

"You don't have to lie to me."

"It's true. I'm not saying it to make you feel better."

Relenting, Gil finally gave her a look. Once again, she'd borrowed *Mamm*'s old coat, bundling it around her to ward off the cold. The strings of her *kapp* were tied firmly beneath her chin to keep the breeze from snatching it away.

"I feel like I'm walking through quicksand." Sucking in a breath, he felt icy air scorch his lungs. "I want to do better, faster. I want to understand all the words."

She angled her chin with firm insistence. Despite the biting cold nipping at her rosy cheeks, her eyes sparkled with a warmth that defied the wintry evening. "Learning to read takes time. It's like when you work with your horses—patience is the key to taming them, ain't that so?"

Gil's throat tightened as emotion welled up. "I want to read the Bible without stumbling over every word. I want to feel the words in my heart, not just hear them."

Florene placed a reassuring hand on his arm. Her touch was a balm to his restlessness. "You can and you will. We'll walk this path together, one word at a time, one page at a time. So don't quit on me now."

Gratitude filled him. It felt strange to reveal the vulnerability he rarely shared. But it also felt good that someone understood. She was so insistent. He didn't want to disappoint her.

"I'm not giving up," he promised.

Chapter Seven

The first rays of dawn spilled through the cracks in the wooden shutters, casting dim shadows through the simple bedroom.

Florene stirred in her narrow bed, feeling a wave of nausea twist her insides. Eyes fluttering open, she pressed a hand to her stomach. "Oh, not again."

Lying quietly, she waited for the spell to pass. The persistent sensation lingered, wrapping itself around her like an invisible shroud.

At first, she'd believed the faint queasiness settling in the pit of her stomach was caused by Zane's cruel abuse. But as the months had passed, she'd begun to sense the changes in her body were something more than stress.

A wave of emotions surged through her. Discovering she was pregnant had been terrifying. It had forced her to acknowledge the truth she'd avoided far too long. The relationship she found herself trapped in was no longer just about her. She couldn't subject her unborn child to the same toxic environment that had cast a shadow over her life for too many years.

Fighting the knots in her stomach, Florene pushed aside the covers and stood on shaky legs. Her simple nightgown clung to her.

The room swayed ever so slightly as she tried to take a few steps. The world seemed to be in a gentle spin, as if reality itself were trying to lull her into a surreal dreamscape. Stumbling to the vanity, she dipped a hand into the basin. A splash of water helped cool her feverish skin.

Regaining her balance, Florene stared into the mirror. Stunningly, her image had changed through the last few days. Bruises were fading, and the redness of the scrapes was slowly replaced with the glow of rejuvenated skin. Lines of stress and unhappiness had eased, returning tranquility to her gaze. Despite the nausea, she looked healthier than she had in a long while.

As she looked at her reflection, new feelings blossomed inside, gentle yet powerful—oh, how she'd missed the contentment of simple living!

A thought came out of nowhere. *I want to stay.*

But how could she? To fully return to the community, she'd have to visit the bishop, repent and rejoin the church. She'd also have to believe in *Gott*, accepting the words in the Bible as the way and the truth. To be baptized and fully vested in the church, she'd also have to give a testament of faith.

Uncertainty clenched her insides suddenly. She wasn't sure if she'd ever been a believer—or if she ever could be. Growing up, she'd attended church most of her life. But she'd barely listened to the sermons, disregarding them the moment services had ended. Dry, dusty words in an old book meant little when one was young and full of curiosity about the *Englisch* and their ways.

Time and experience had tempered her journey outside of her sheltered community. It had also revealed a hollow void inside, the emptiness and decay of a life lived without any sort of spiritual connection.

Her gaze wandered across the room. On the nightstand lay the Bible Almeda had loaned her. The cover, once vibrant, had softened into a gentle patina from countless times of use.

A long time had passed since she'd sought the Lord. *Maybe it's time.*

Returning to the bed, she lit a lamp before sitting down. She opened the book and ran her fingers across a stray page, feeling the texture of the paper. Then, settling on a passage, she attempted to immerse herself in the teachings that had guided mankind through countless generations.

Blessed are they that hear the word of God and keep it.

As she read the passage from Luke 11:28, a

sense of unease crept over her. She'd often heard the word of *Gott* but hadn't abided.

Growing uneasy, she read on. But comfort and clarity seemed elusive, slipping through her grasp like grains of sand. She longed to make a spiritual connection with the Lord, but she felt nothing. Clouded with doubt and worry, her own thoughts kept intruding.

Tears welled as guilt swamped her. "Why don't I feel anything?" she pleaded, her voice barely audible. She knew she'd sinned, and the questions of acceptance and redemption loomed large. The weight of tradition and the fear of judgment from her community intensified her internal struggle.

Silence followed as her ears strained for a divine response. But the room remained hushed, the only sound the gentle rustling of a breeze outside. The lack of a profound revelation left her with a sense of emptiness, as if her prayers were merely echoes into nothing.

Was the Lord turning away because of her transgressions? Did the *boppli* growing within her womb separate her from the divine grace she so desperately sought? Was the child—a gift from *Gott* though conceived outside the sanctity of marriage—keeping her from walking in grace?

But no answers came.

A fresh twist of nausea gripped her. She'd been unable to eat the night before, and now she needed something to ease her stomach.

Laying the Bible aside, she rose. She washed up for the day and put on one of the borrowed dresses from Nella. Slipping into a sweater to keep the morning chill away, she crept down the narrow hallway, her steps soft, careful not to disturb the slumbering household. Up all night with their fussy *boppli*, Nella and Eli were usually the last ones to rise in the morning.

The aroma of baking and brewed *kaffee* from the kitchen greeted her as she came downstairs. A fire crackled in the hearth, sending its warm illumination throughout the large open living space.

Almeda's hands moved gracefully as she kneaded more dough on the well-worn cabinet top, humming to herself. The filtered light streaming through the kitchen window highlighted the flour-dusted air, giving the space an almost ethereal quality. Her apron, worn and stained with the marks of countless meals prepared, spoke volumes of a life dedicated to the art of nurturing through food. Despite her injury, she was determined to get around and keep her *haus* in order.

Florene couldn't help but pause to appreciate the scene before her. She liked the older woman. Almeda read the Bible daily, and often spent her free time working on projects that would benefit others in the community. With nimble fingers, she knitted up scarves and hats and sent them to the church to be distributed to those less fortunate.

"Guten morgen," Florene greeted.

Almeda glanced up from her work. "Wasn't expecting you up early since you weren't feeling well last night."

She offered a wan smile. "I'm better today." The previous evening hadn't been a good one at all. Her morning sickness also came at night. Feeling woozy, she hadn't been able to take a single bite of the hearty beef stew and biscuits that had been their dinner.

Concern wrinkled Almeda's brow. "You look flushed. Hope you're not coming down with something. There was a virus going around. Viola Ratch caught it a few weeks ago so bad it put her off her feet."

"I don't think I have it," Florene said, mustering the courage to continue her deception. But her trembling legs refused to hold her weight any longer. Moving toward the table, she sank into a chair. "Just need a cup of tea to settle my stomach."

"I'll make it for you." Wiping her hands on a clean cloth, Almeda filled the kettle with water before setting it atop the stove. Her movements were slow as she hadn't yet learned to navigate well with her cane. "Sure hope this cast comes off soon."

Florene started to rise. "Let me."

The older woman waved her back. "It does me no *gut* to sit and wait for my foot to heal. I'm used to doing things, and I'm going to do them.

Just takes me longer, so bear with me." Reaching into the cupboard, she took down a tin. "I've got dried ginger and lemon right here." Spooning out the blend, she added a generous dollop of honey. "Chases away the bitter." Pouring boiling water into the stoneware mug, she carried it to the table. "Nella often felt ill before she had Isaiah. This made her feel better."

Florene averted her gaze, fidgeting with the hem of her apron. No reason to give herself away. *"Danke."* Steam rose from the cup, carrying an earthy scent that tickled the senses. She took a sip, feeling the warmth travel down her throat.

"Is *gut*?"

"Ja."

"Go ahead. Drink it all."

She did as she was told. The citrus-infused brew chased away the queasiness. "That helps a lot."

"I knew it would." A glint of knowing came into Almeda's eyes. "I may be old, but I know when a young woman is carrying."

Florene froze. Her pulse quickened as a tumultuous mix of emotions threatened to upend her fragile composure. Her secret weighed heavily on her heart, but the fear of judgment and gossip held her captive.

"Nein," she said, shaking her head. "I'm not."

"If you say so," Almeda responded.

Swamped with guilt, Florene covered her

mouth with a hand. Continuing the deception wasn't the path she wanted to walk. Dishonesty and shame were no way to bring her precious *youngie* into this world.

"I—I'm sorry. I lied." Pulse turning to a dull thud, she swallowed hard, mustering the courage to continue. "Please, don't tell anyone."

"Not my place to share your business, but—" Silvery brows rose in a knowing manner. "You aren't going to be able to keep that little one secret much longer." Softened by wisdom, her voice carried the weight of experience and compassion.

The burden of uncertainty pressed hard. "I know. Just as soon as the weather clears, I'll leave."

"And go where?"

"I don't know," she said, shaking her head. "But I can't stay. If Zane finds me, there could be trouble."

"This fella you're running from…is he the *daadi*?"

"Ja." Dropping her hands, Florene clasped them tightly in her lap. "But I don't want him to know. Ever."

A hush settled over her statement. A long minute ticked by, and then another.

Breaking the silence, Almeda placed a firm hand on her shoulder. "Gilead would look after you both." A quiver of hope touched the older woman's lips. "He is a gentle man, and hardworking."

Caught by surprise, Florene found her breath hitching. "I'm not ready," she blurted, her words stumbling over each other. The notion of becoming anyone's *fraa* sent shivers down her spine, even as fear of the unknown shoved her closer to an emotional breakdown.

Still, like a faraway echo, the suggestion lingered, presenting a tantalizing question.

Would marrying the shy Amish bachelor be the answer she was searching for?

In the dim early morning light, Gil stood in the training corral. Needing a break from the walls around him, he'd set to work early. His hat shaded his eyes, its brim casting a shadow on his brow. Before him, a wild mustang, its coat a cluttered mix of blacks and browns, nervously pawed the ground. The untamed energy of the creature was palpable.

Snorting and stamping, the large stallion was magnificent. The air hummed with tension. Although it was too cold to do any real work, the deep snow would give him the opportunity to teach the untamed horse to accept his presence and touch.

Snowbanks rose like frozen waves. He plowed through the snow and approached the skittish animal. The mustang's breath formed clouds of steam, and mistrust emanated from its glinting eyes. In the wild, it had been chased down and trapped against its will.

Using his size and bulk, Gil kept the horse cornered. As he extended a hand toward the wild horse, the animal's nostrils flared with defiance. Snorting a warning, the horse reared up to defend itself, forelegs beating the air.

Gil dodged the danger, keeping his distance until the horse came back down. "Now, now, I'm not going to hurt you." Keeping in mind that *Gott* commanded men to regard the lives of all creatures, he refused to be cruel to animals. He'd never used a whip on any creature, and never would. Nor would he give a horse or mule a burden too heavy to bear. He knew the condition of all livestock on the farm, giving each care and comfort.

With quiet confidence, he approached again, every step measured and deliberate. He never employed brutal methods. Nor did he use ropes. Instead, he chose to convey a quiet power, an aura of calm.

Muscles rippling, the horse again recoiled, hooves scraping the snowy ground. It didn't trust men and didn't want to be trapped.

Undeterred, Gil spoke in hushed tones, his voice one of reassurance. Summoning patience, he continued his approach. He sensed the rhythm of the horse's fear, the pulse of its wild heart. Each movement, each breath, was met with a steady presence. The deep drifts acted as a hobble, slowing the stallion's attempt to avoid him. Refusing to let the horse pass, he blocked the animal's escape. Finding rhythm in the chaos, he kept the stallion cornered, allowing it to expend its nervous energy.

"This doesn't have to be hard," he soothed, speaking in a quiet voice. Sweat dripped from his brow, not from exertion, but from the emotional investment in this untamed spirit. "All I want to do is pet you."

The horse kicked and bucked without restraint.

Gil refused to relent. The choreography continued, each movement deliberate and purposeful. Staggered by the deep snow, the stallion began to tire. The wildfire in its eyes flickered, replaced by a glimmer of surrender. Body heaving, it eased its resistance.

And then it was over.

"Got tired, did you?" Extending his arm, he stretched out a hand. "It's okay. I won't hurt you." The first touch, when it came, was gentle. His fingers moved through the coarse mane with a tenderness that belied his immense strength. At that moment, a connection formed as the horse yielded to his authority. The barrier of mistrust that held it captive crumbled. The mustang's head bowed, not to dominance but a newfound trust.

"Hey!" Bundled in her borrowed coat, Florene stood outside the gate. Hands adorned with woolen mittens, she raised the thermos she carried. "Thought you'd like something hot to drink."

Gil offered a quick wave. "Be right there." Giving the mustang's long neck a final pet, he made his way through the drifts. He slipped through the gate and locked it. After he took a break, he'd dry the horse down before returning it to the herd.

Head tipping back, she smiled a greeting. The chill painted her cheeks with a natural blush. "Seems like I always find you here."

He shrugged. "Only place I like to be nowadays."

She glanced past him. "My *daed* used to say it took a special touch to tame a wild horse. From what I've seen, you have it."

The compliment warmed him. "Patience is the key. These animals may be wild, but they can sense a man's intentions."

"You've got a real gift."

Gil cleared his throat, trying to deflect the attention away from himself. Humility conflicted with the praise he was receiving. He wasn't accustomed to being the center of anyone's attention. Especially when that someone was a pretty *fraulein*. "Oh, there's a few that have gotten the better of me. Couldn't break them, so I sold them off to the rodeo."

"Levi—Gail's *ehmann*, you know—used to ride broncs."

"*Ja*. I recall Levi mentioned that a time or two,"

he laughed. "I also recall he said he didn't miss the bumps and scrapes that come with getting thrown."

"Hard to believe it's been three years since I've seen everyone. I sure do miss them."

"I'm sure your *familie* wants to see you and know you're okay."

Florene's breath quickened, visible puffs of warmth contrasting against the frozen backdrop. "I can't."

"You still think that fella of yours is going to cause trouble if he finds out?"

Muscles tensed along her temples. "I don't think it. I *know* it. I can't go home. Zane told me he'd k—" The color suddenly drained from her cheeks, leaving behind a pale canvas that spoke volumes of the emotions that held her captive. "Can we not talk about it?"

Gil backed off. She'd been abused. He knew that. She was scared. He knew that, too. All he could do was offer her space, a place to heal as she tried to rebuild her life.

"I could sure use that hot drink," he said, rubbing his hands together to chase away the numbness in his fingers. Despite the thickness of his leather gloves, the chill was beginning to seep in.

Somber mood breaking, her eyes brightened. "Oh, *ja*, of course. Almost forgot I had it." Slipping off her mittens, she uncapped the thermos. Steam curled into the air as she poured the dark brew into the matching cup. "You like it black, right?"

He accepted the hot drink. "I do. *Danke*." The enticing aroma filled the space between them. He took a sip, savoring the warmth that spread through him. "I appreciate you bringing it out."

"I like helping."

"I know *Mamm* likes having the extra hands." It was true. Florene had taken over the chores that were difficult for someone with a cane to handle. "And I know Nella and Eli appreciate having a break from Isaiah."

"He's a lovely baby. Nella's just so nervous with him. She's upset all the time, and that makes him upset, too."

"Eli wants to make her happy, but he doesn't have the money it would take to get a *haus* in Burr Oak."

She looked around. "It's so nice here. You've got lots of places to keep the gardens and animals. I can't imagine what else she'd want."

Gil barely stopped himself from rolling his eyes. "I can't think of a thing Nella doesn't complain about."

A subtle furrow etched Florene's brow. "I remember how spoiled Nella was when we were growing up," she said. "I guess she forgot being satisfied with what you have is better than wanting more."

"Her *daed* always let her have what she wanted. She expects Eli to provide those things now."

"A big *haus* and whatnot are just stuff. Useless stuff." Florene's gaze carried the weight of knowing. "What counts is having people who love you and want to share your life, through the *gut* things and the bad. It's sad Nella doesn't see how blessed she really is." As she spoke, her shoulders hunched forward, an involuntary manifestation of the burdens she felt pressing down in her own life.

Gil blew out an exasperated breath. "*Gott* will have to change her ways. No one else can." As he spoke, the breeze kicked up, bringing in a fresh rush of frigid air.

Florene shivered, pulling her coat tighter around her, attempting to shield herself from the biting wind that seemed determined to find any gap in the layers. Despite the visible discomfort of the cold, there was a quiet strength in her demeanor. "A woman's heart can change." Her voice, so soft, held a quiver of longing. "I know mine has." Going silent, she gazed into the distance.

A hush fell over the solemn moment. Her stillness invited contemplation.

Gil visually traced the delicate arc of her cheeks and the fine wisps of hair peeking out from under her prayer *kapp*. Unlike Nella, who often gave way to bouts of petulance and gestures of selfishness, Florene had a giving nature. She was grateful for the smallest act of kindness and worked to return it tenfold.

But that hadn't always been true.

Gossip around town frequently painted her as flighty and irresponsible. She'd been known to skip church and other community events. Come *rumspringa*, she'd turned outright disrespectful, rejecting her Amish upbringing with harsh declarations. Her rebellious streak had often made her the subject of hushed conversations and disapproving glances.

However her time in the *Englisch* world seemed to have tempered her manners. Florene was doing her best to fit in. In his eyes, she'd changed. Simply by the way she acted, he could tell the weight of past choices pressed hard on her conscience. She clearly longed to be back among Plain folks, to feel the security of their way of life and the comfort of shared values.

Stirring, she shook off her solemn mood. "I promised Almeda I'd be back to help with breakfast," she said. "I hope you're hungry. There'll be biscuits and sausage gravy. Oh, and I'm making sweet potato hash to go with it."

Nodding, Gil handed over the empty cup. "Sounds *gut*."

Taking a few steps, Florene suddenly stopped and turned around. "You'll come inside? Soon?"

"*Ja*. As soon as I get the horse put up."

A faint smile tugged her lips. "I'll see you

then." She turned again, walking away. This time she didn't look back.

Gil watched her go. Reaching the porch, she trotted up the steps before disappearing through the back door. Emptiness crept in. So did his thoughts. What would it be like to share moments like this for the rest of their lives? Florene had no *ehmann*, no husband to take care of her. Once again, it was easy to imagine a future as her companion in life's journey.

Right there, the world around him dissolved. His pulse skipped to a new beat, delivering a cascade of sensations he'd never known before. The connection wasn't a sudden spark; it was a gradual illumination, like the sunrise painting the horizon in hues of yellow and pink. More than joy, or surprise, the sensation was indescribable—and instantly recognized by every man who'd ever walked the earth.

Shifting in his place, Gil swallowed hard. Was this how love happened?

A sense of vulnerability washed over him. He'd never had romantic notions toward any female. Wasn't even sure how it was supposed to feel.

Snorting, he lowered his head. *She wouldn't want a scruffy fella like me.*

Chapter Eight

The kitchen echoed with the clinking of utensils against the ceramic plates, a melody of the morning routine. Everyone had eaten well, enjoying the hearty breakfast. The Lord had provided a comforting, nourishing meal.

Famished, Gil savored each bite with gratitude. The food served was some of his favorites and he'd eaten two servings. Swirling the last of his biscuit through the gravy, he swallowed down the morsel. The spicy homemade sausage had given the gravy just the right flavor, complementing the fluffy scrambled eggs and hash Florene had whipped up. Rather than using regular potatoes, she'd used sweet potatoes. Fried in butter and caramelized in brown sugar with a dash of cinnamon, cloves and nutmeg, the dish balanced out the savory selections. A mug of ice-cold buttermilk was the perfect way to top it all off.

Noticing his empty plate, Florene pushed away from the table and hurried to the stove. She returned with a platter of biscuits. "There's a drop of gravy left if you want it," she offered.

Gil chuckled, gesturing toward his stomach. "You've just about stuffed me full."

"You sure?" she prodded, extending the platter again.

He waved his hands. "I couldn't eat another bite."

Eli held out his empty plate. "I'll have another biscuit and the rest of that gravy, if you don't mind."

"Certainly," she said, setting to the task.

Gil watched as Florene moved effortlessly between the stove and the table, flitting around the kitchen with the sure steps of a woman who belonged. Throughout the morning, she'd overseen breakfast with a steady hand. Her attentiveness spared *Mamm* the work it took to get the food on the table.

Danke, Lord, for guiding her here, he prayed, grateful for her presence. Now that she'd settled in, Florene had seamlessly woven herself into the fabric of their lives. Her vibrant personality filled the home with a welcome, new warmth.

Nella scooped up the last bite on her plate. "I'll have more of that sweet hash, if there's any."

"*Ja*, there is." Obliging, Florene refilled her dish with a smile. "Is there anything else you'd care to have while I'm up?"

"*Nein,*" Nella said, spooning up the delicious

treat. "Though I will say I'm absolutely in love with this hash."

"It's my *grossmammi's* recipe," Florene replied, stacking the empty dishes in the sink. "She only made it for special occasions."

Mamm beamed with satisfaction at the sight of her family happily nourished. "*Danke* for sharing it with us."

Florene ran hot water into the sink. "I enjoyed having a chance to make it," she said, wiping her hands on a dishrag. "It's been a long time since I've cooked on a wood-burning stove with real cast-iron pots and pans. I'd forgotten how that brings out all the flavors."

"I wouldn't have anything else," *Mamm* agreed with a nod. "Those newfangled appliances Nella thinks she wants just don't seem like they'd do half as well."

"Oh, pish!" Nella snapped back. "Why, I grew up having all those things, and they were fine for my *mamm*." Tipping her chin in an arrogant manner, she added, "*Daed* made sure she had all the conveniences. The *Ordnung* says we may have them, you know, and I don't see why we shouldn't."

"I've been using that woodstove for decades," *Mamm* said. "It's reliable and there's no reason to change."

Gil winced. The morning, which had been so pleasant, immediately disintegrated. Nella and

Mamm argued frequently about updating the *haus* with modern appliances. The conflict was beginning to wear everyone down.

"Can we not ruin the morning?" he pleaded, attempting to mediate.

"Propane is more efficient," Eli insisted, taking his *ehefrau's* side. "It's a clean burning fuel, and we wouldn't have to spend so much time chopping wood and tending the fire."

Mamm's expression tightened as she put down her fork. "I'm not having any in my kitchen."

The debate continued. Eli and Nella passionately defended their respective positions. *Mamm* stubbornly put her foot down, refusing to relent.

Sniffling, Nella suddenly burst into tears. Dropping her spoon, she pushed her food away. "I hate this dreary old place," she declared dramatically. "It's dark and depressing!"

Roused by his mother's distress, Isaiah suddenly burst into loud wails.

Nella rose to scoop her infant out of his bassinet. "Now see what you've done," she flung at her mother-in-law. "I get upset and Isaiah gets fussy. It's not *gut* for either of us." She looked to Florene as if in desperation. "You've lived in the *Englisch* world. Surely you wouldn't want to cook on that dreadful thing every day of the week."

Florene didn't hesitate. "I'd cook on it every day of my life if I could," she said, turning toward the stalwart old stove. "I know it's more work, but

I believe it connects us to our past and reminds us that humble is how *Gott* expects us to live."

"*Ach*, that's exactly how I feel," *Mamm* said, nodding with approval.

Holding the baby close, Nella disagreed. "It would be so much nicer not to have to do so much cleaning. And the ash isn't *gut* for Isaiah's lungs, either."

Eli wiped his mouth, brushing crumbs out of his beard. "It wouldn't hurt to consider a few changes," he grumbled, refusing to acquiesce. His expression shifted from mild annoyance to certainty. "Now that I have a *fraa* and *youngie*, I should be the one making the decisions about how we should live."

Gil bristled, unable to tolerate disrespect toward an elder. "Don't get high-handed," he warned. "This is still *Mamm*'s *haus* and you'll be mindful how you speak."

Scorn crept into Eli's face. "It's the truth I'm speaking, and you know it." His nostrils flared as defiance visibly tightened his jaw. "I'm the one who has to look out for this *familie* now. Our future is in my hands, and I'll decide how it'll be."

Brother glared at brother, the weight of the disagreement pressing down from all sides.

"Enough," *Mamm* demanded, looking between them. "If your *daed* was here, there'd be none of this nonsense." A tremble shook her frail body as she remembered the husband she'd lost. "*Kann nicht mehr viel ertragen,"* she finished, burying her face in her hands. *My heart can't take much more*, she'd said.

A knot tightened in Gil's chest. Respecting her grief, he backed off. It was best to let it go and keep the peace. Not that it would last very long. Except for Isaiah, Eli's marriage to Nella had sown nothing but strife and dissatisfaction. A spoiled city girl didn't belong in the country. Ten months in and everyone's nerves were stretched to the breaking point.

The kitchen, once filled with warmth, now felt cold and fractured. The crackling of the old woodstove seemed to underscore the tension.

"I didn't mean to step out of place," Eli allowed. "But there's nothing wrong with thinking about the needs of my wife and child."

Mamm dabbed her misty eyes. "Ecclesiastes tells us there is a time for every matter," she conceded. "Things should be settled between you and your brother."

"I agree," Eli prompted. "It'd best happen before another *boppli* comes along."

"I'd like to know Isaiah has a secure future," Nella chimed in.

Florene gave the persuasive duo an uncomfortable glance. The look on her face said she had something on her mind. Instead of speaking, she shook her head before turning to the dishes in the sink. "I'll get these done," she murmured, setting to the task of cleaning up with quiet determination.

Gil folded his arms across his chest, aware of Eli's subtle wheedling. He wasn't so willing to concede, but anything he said would most likely fall on deaf ears. *Daed*'s passing had widened the divide in his relationship with his *bruder*.

A sudden eruption of chaos shattered the moment. A series of sharp guttural barks echoed through the air.

Everyone froze, exchanging worried glances. All arguing was laid aside. A new danger had taken its place.

"What in the world?" Gil jumped to his feet, rushing toward the back door.

"Bet it's a coyote!" Eli exclaimed.

Mamm gave a worried look. "They usually don't come this close to the *haus*."

Nella clung tighter to Isaiah. "This is why I hate living in the country," she snapped to her husband. "Between the rattlesnakes and coyotes, it isn't safe to step outside."

"I'll take care of the varmint," Eli promised, reaching for the rifle hung on pegs above the back door. Reserved for protecting livestock, the weapon was necessary for keeping predators at bay.

Mamm's solemn nod conveyed her understanding of the need to deal with the threat. "I hate harming any of *Gott*'s creatures, but it's necessary."

"We used to fight to keep them from killing the cattle," Florene added. "It's dangerous when they pack up for hunting."

Gil's heart thudded faster, sending a rush of adrenaline through his veins. "Doesn't sound like a pack, but even one coyote is too many." Anxious to scare away the invader, he didn't even bother to put on his coat. Barreling across the porch, he fought his way through the deep drifts. The chill of the day enveloped him, but he barely noticed it. All he focused on was the shadowy figure dashing around the corral, moving with unsettling agility. The horses, usually calm and placid, were in a frenzied state.

Eli followed at his heels. Face etched with determination, he raised the rifle toward the threat. "Just be still a minute," he grated, taking aim at the moving target.

Seeing the two men, the animal momentarily froze. Suddenly, it set out at a dead run, sprinting toward them.

Eli's finger tightened on the trigger. "I've got him!"

Just as Eli prepared to fire, a flicker of recognition flashed through Gil's mind. He squinted, recognizing not the menacing silhouette of a coyote but the black-and-white fur of their neighbor's dog. Without meaning to, they were about to injure an innocent animal.

With a swift motion, he grabbed his brother's arm, forcing the rifle downward. "Hold it, Eli! It's Donny Reese's dog," he cried, his voice urgent yet filled with relief.

The tension in the air dissipated as quickly as it had surfaced.

Eli lowered the rifle, breathing out the weight of what could have been. "I didn't know." He gave a look of embarrassment, and gratitude for narrowly avoiding a tragic mistake.

"It's Blu." Kneeling, Gil put out a hand. The dog hovered a few feet away, scared to come closer. "Come on, boy, come here."

Recognizing his voice, the husky approached. Tail tucked between its legs, its brown eyes pleaded for mercy. It appeared thin and scraggly, and its matted coat bore the difficulty of a long journey.

"It isn't right for Donny to let his dog roam," Eli spat back. "He needs to keep it on his property."

Gil shook his head. Seeing the canine's pitiful state was like a punch in the gut. "Donny loves this dog. If Blu's running loose, something's wrong. Bad wrong."

"Never was much good to that old drunkard," Eli grumbled back, blowing out a disgusted breath. He prodded the dog with the butt of his rifle. "Set that dog loose and let it go on its way. It looks like it's near to dying anyway."

Gil rose. He gave Blu a worried glance. The dog was looking for help from humans. "I'm not going to do that." Slipping his fingers into the canine's worn collar, he began to guide it toward the barn. The animal needed shelter, food and water.

Eli jogged to catch up. "Wait!" he demanded. "Where are you going?"

Disregarding the question, Gil hastened his steps. The severity of the storms and bone-chilling temperatures heightened his concern for the well-being of his neighbor. It didn't matter that the man was an *Englischer*, or that he had a reputation when it came to hoisting the whisky bottle. A fellow human might be in trouble.

"Help me hitch the buggy," he ordered. "I'm heading over to check on Donny."

"Think you can make it?" Eli asked, eyeing the deep drifts. "Seems a little risky if you ask me."

Gil didn't hesitate. "I can," he said. "And I will."

Traveling in an unheated vehicle on a winter day wasn't comfortable. It was downright miserable.

Florene shivered, pulling the folds of her coat tighter. Despite the scarf wound around her head and face and heavy leather gloves on her hands, she was chilled to the bone. The blanket spread over her lap didn't help much, either.

"I'd forgotten how cold these things can get," she commented through chattering teeth.

Bundled beside her, Gil guided the horse with calm expertise. "I can turn around. It's no trouble to go by myself."

She shook her head. *"Nein,"* she said. "I'm fine."

"It was nice of you to offer to go," he said, keeping his eyes straight ahead.

Florene gripped the seat as the buggy rolled over a rough patch in the road. "It's nice to have a chance to get out. Felt like everyone was getting a little tense at breakfast."

"Happens when people are all cooped up." He cast a look toward the leaden sky. Thankfully, no more snow had fallen, but the clouds were determined to stay put. Their presence cast a gray pall over the land. "Be happy when this weather clears."

"Me, too." Smoothing the folds out of the blanket, she broached the subject dividing the household. "Doesn't it bother you how Eli treats everyone?"

Gil's brow furrowed even as a grimace twisted his mouth. "He's always been like that."

"Doesn't it make you angry?"

"I could be ugly back, but it won't do me no *gut*," he said, offering a brief smile. "And worrying doesn't add an hour to my life. I'll pray harder and let *Gott* do the work." The rhythmic creaking of the buggy seemed to underscore the weight of his words.

Florene gave him a long look. His confidence in the Lord was unwavering. No matter the problem, he believed his prayers would be answered.

Her gaze dropped to her hands folded in her lap. *If only I did...*

But she still felt nothing when she prayed, and she continued to question the very foundations of the religion that had shaped her existence.

Emotion tightened its grip. Her lack of belief sat heavy on her conscience. Unwilling to delve into the disturbing feelings, she looked down the road. When they'd set out on their journey, Gil had indicated the trip would be a short one. The Reese property was a few miles down a back utility road, he'd said. Shouldn't take no more than half an hour to reach. As if to prove his words true, the horse plowed through the drifts without hesitation.

Sensing trouble, Gil had loaded the vehicle down with supplies. He'd brought along a little of everything—food, medicine, extra blankets and tools. Fed and rested, the dog he'd rescued rode comfortably in the back seat. Half-starved, the poor animal had gobbled down its meal without hesitation.

The ride went on, broken only by the heaving efforts of the horse and squeaking buggy wheels.

The sturdy animal struggled against the snow, its breath coming out in clouds as it plodded forward.

Suddenly, the mare stumbled, sinking into a particularly stubborn drift. The buggy lurched and then came to a stop, wedged in place.

Florene's pulse sped up. "I think we're stuck," she said, voice trembling.

Gil glanced at her. "I'll get us out." Eyes filled with determination, he climbed down and trudged through the knee-deep snow.

Steam rising from her heaving flanks, the horse let out a nervous whinny.

Florene tracked his every move. "Is she okay?" The danger of being trapped and freezing to death was something she didn't want to think about.

"She's fine," he called back, patting the horse's neck. "We just got ourselves into a deep patch. Going to have to get ourselves out." Bracing himself against the side, he pushed with all his might.

Florene clutched the reins he'd abandoned. "Be careful," she called, fearing he would fall beneath the wheels. The path ahead seemed impassable.

Gil stayed on his feet. His muscles strained against the weight, but he refused to give up. Tugging against her harness, the mare struggled to regain her footing. Man and beast worked together, sharing the resolve to overcome the challenge. With each heave and push, the heavy vehicle inched forward.

Minutes ticked away as they forged ahead.

Progress was slow, but steady. Finally, after one last tremendous effort from Gil, the wheels found traction.

Gil hurried back to the buggy, panting heavily. "Think we're over the worst of it." Breath forming clouds in the frigid air, he reclaimed his seat. "We're almost there."

Florene allowed herself to relax. "I hope so."

"Didn't think it would take this long, but the snow is deeper than I thought. Sure hope no one is out on the highway. If a horse can't handle it, nothing else on wheels can."

With renewed vigor, they continued their mission. The journey felt endless, the weather seeming to conspire against them.

"You know Donny Reese well?" she threw out to get the conversation going again.

"Suppose I do." Lines of contemplation etched Gil's face as he gathered his facts. "Been neighbors for as long as I can remember."

She nodded. Most everyone in Burr Oak did know Donny. With his disheveled appearance and a perpetual odor of cheap liquor clinging to him, the *Englischer* was a pariah in the eyes of the townsfolk. His scandalous marriage to the former bishop's niece had set tongues to wagging.

"Guess no one will ever get over him eloping with Hannah Glick."

"They did all right for a while. Shame everything fell apart for him after Hannah passed."

Shaking his head, Gil made a clicking sound with his tongue, urging the horse to hasten its steps. The buggy rolled a little faster. "Kind of sad her daughter ended up in a bad way, too."

Florene winced, thankful the knitted scarf covered half her face. A little over three years ago, her sisters had temporarily fostered Mary Reese's newborn. Alone and scared, the girl had suffered a mental breakdown after giving birth, requiring emergency hospitalization. The day social services took the infant away had deeply affected everyone involved.

"It was a shame," she whispered, her voice soft and reflective.

"I'm glad the girl was able to move on," he said. "Last I heard, she went to live with a cousin on her *mamm*'s side. I hope she was able to find some happiness."

"Me, too." As she struggled to control the turmoil within, unbidden tears misted her vision. She blinked hard to clear them away.

Unaware of her emotion, Gil glanced at the dog resting in the back seat. "I can't imagine why Donny let Blu get in such bad shape. Last time I saw him he was doing okay. He helps me out sometimes, doing odd jobs and such." Releasing a frosty breath, he rubbed the tip of his nose. Sneaking through his scarf, the chill had reddened his cheeks and ears. "Eli doesn't like him, but I don't mind him as long as he stays sober."

Florene looked down at the basket of food tucked by her feet. Eli had made his opinions on the matter clear. He'd argued over every item Almeda had taken out of her cupboards. At least Nella had had the sense to pitch in and help instead of passing judgment on an unfortunate soul.

Unwilling to let Gil make the trip alone, Florene had volunteered to accompany him. No one knew what might be waiting down the road. If there was trouble, more than one pair of hands would surely be needed. Plus, she was desperate to escape the disharmony simmering in the household. Eli's wheedling and whining were getting on her nerves. Nella, too, had become tiresome.

Between the two of them, Florene felt the couple deserved each other. She'd never met a more selfish pair.

Just the way I used to be.

The man sitting beside her wasn't like that. Gil was willing to lend anyone a hand. Instead of grumbling about the inconvenience of helping his *Englisch* neighbor, he'd hitched his strongest mare to the buggy. No matter how bad the storm was, he was determined to make the trek. Nothing would change his mind.

A living testament to the values he held dear, he allowed his actions to speak louder than any sermon. In him. Florene saw a reflection of the human being she aspired to be. He'd truly inspired her to change, to be more selfless and compassionate. She intended to follow the path, wherever it might take her.

She sneaked another look at Gil. Almeda's earlier suggestion that she give him a chance to care for her and the *boppli* still lingered in the back of her mind. His strong work ethic and commitment to his community would be valued by any sensible woman. The stability and security he offered were undeniable—and his yearning for *youngies* was evident. Yet, even as she considered the possibility of a future with him, a longing for a connection that transcended obligation tugged at her. She had no doubt that Gil's intentions would be pure. But the question of whether she could reciprocate the depth of emotion he offered hung like a delicate thread in the air. An Amish partnership was expected to last a lifetime. She didn't want to marry for convenience. She wanted to marry for love.

Truth be told, she wasn't certain she could summon the affection necessary for a loving partnership. The idea of opening herself up to another man was terrifying on so many levels. Yes, she'd known Gil all her life. But did she *really* know him?

Turning down another little side road, Gil guided the buggy through an open gate. "Looks like we made it." He pulled to a stop and set the hand brake. Buggy stable, he jumped to the ground.

"You coming?" he asked, holding out a hand.

Florene slid the blanket off her lap and grabbed a handful of her skirt. Slipping her hand into his, she allowed him to help her step down. *"Danke."*

Blu jumped down, eager to be home. A low whine broke from the husky's throat. "Hold on, boy." Catching the dog by its collar, Gil took a few steps forward, surveying the lay of the property.

Looking around, Florene clutched her coat tighter. The white, pristine snow contrasted sharply with the rusting skeletons of broken-down vehicles scattered across the unkempt yard. The once-sturdy picket fence lay partially buried beneath the drifts, sagging under the weight of neglect. Bearing the burden of time and weather, the *haus* wasn't in much better shape, either.

The squall kicked up, adding an eerie chill to the decay surrounding them. The homestead had a sense of abandonment. The desolation was unnerving. Whatever life the place once had appeared to have withered away.

As the bitter gusts tugged at her scarf, Florene looked toward the house for any signs of habitation. No smoke emanated from the stone chimney, nor was there any light to be seen shining from within. "He's got no fire burning."

"I hope he's not drinking again. That whisky isn't *gut* for anyone."

An exchange of worried glances passed between them.

"Come on." Keeping a hold on the dog's collar, Gil trudged through the knee-deep snow toward the front door. Blu fought to escape and run ahead.

Following at a slower pace, Florene kept behind him. She hated to think about what they might discover.

As they stepped up on the porch, the uneven surface creaked beneath Gil's weight. "Anyone home?" he called, knocking with a heavy hand.

The sound echoed through the hollow space within, eliciting no immediate response.

Blu whined, anxiously pawing the door. Sensing something inside, he suddenly broke into a series of loud barks.

Gil rapped again, harder and more insistent. "You there, Donny?" His voice carried notes of apprehension.

A lock turned. Someone inside cracked the door open. Half a face peered out. "Who's there?"

Gil leaned in. "You know me, Donny," he said, holding the eager dog at bay. "I've come to check on you."

The door opened wider, revealing a man dressed in faded jeans and a flannel shirt.

Florene's hand flew to her mouth, stifling a gasp. She'd never seen a human being in such bad shape. Eyes unfocused, the thin figure shivered beneath the blanket drawn around his shoulders. His feet were bare. Despair clung to him like a shroud.

The poor man struggled to hold himself upright but failed. Legs unable to hold his weight, he sagged against the doorframe. "B-been feelin' bad," he slurred through a gasp. "Think I got the flu."

Chapter Nine

Gil's calloused hands gripped the handle of the well-worn ax. The crisp sound of metal meeting wood echoed through the wintry landscape. His muscles flexed with each deliberate strike. Small clouds of sawdust danced in the air. The urgency of the task fueled his determination, and beads of sweat formed on his brow despite the chill. The cold, unyielding and unforgiving, demanded a large supply.

As the pile of split logs grew, so did his sense of accomplishment. The physical exertion brought a warmth that surpassed the biting cold. With the last swing, the ax embedded itself into a particularly stubborn log, sending a satisfying shiver through his tired arms.

But his work was only half done.

Heaving the logs onto a small wagon with practiced efficiency, he grabbed the handle. Rusty wheels creaked as he dragged his burden through the deep snow. Reaching the front porch, he scooped up a load of wood and headed inside.

The dim light of a kerosene lamp illuminated the simple furnishings of the living room. Despite the run-down appearance of the property, the interior was neat. A worn rug covered the wooden floor, and handmade quilts adorned the back of the couch. The hearth, the heart of the home, beckoned as he carefully stacked the firewood near the stone fireplace. Reaching for the poker, he tended the fire, replenishing the fuel that had burned down to cinders. The crackling flames danced to life, casting a warm glow that flickered throughout the room.

"Is that you, Gil?"

He turned toward the kitchen. *"Ja."*

Florene appeared, balancing a tray. The soft glow of the lamp highlighted the determined lines etched on her face. "I've cleaned up as best I can and I've got some food ready," she said, her voice carrying the weight of concern. *"Gut* thing your *mamm* packed that basket full. There's nothing but crumbs in the cupboards."

Gil's gaze shifted toward the sick room where Donny lay bundled in blankets. The Reese family had owned the property for several generations. He couldn't imagine why his neighbor wasn't better prepared for harsh weather. Even though the old farmhouse was wired with electricity and had propane appliances, high winds regularly took down the power lines.

Rising to his feet, he dusted off clinging bits of wood and other small debris. "How is he?"

"Worst case of the flu I've ever seen." Bustling past him, she nudged open the bedroom door. "He needs to eat to get some strength back."

Anxious to check on his friend, Gil followed. The space was dimly lit by a solitary oil lamp hanging from a hook near the bed. The flickering light danced across the pale figure, highlighting the vulnerability etched in his features.

"How're you feeling, Donny?"

The sick man struggled to sit up. "I've had better days." Body racked with fever, he was weak as a newborn calf. His eyes, weary and hollow, held a muted glimmer of gratitude. "Thank you both for comin'."

"Now you lie back and rest," Florene scolded as she set the tray on a small table. "I've got chicken soup and hot tea to help get your strength back." Plumping up the pillows, she tended to him with care, gentle with her words and actions.

"Thought I wasn't going to make it," he said, gratefully sipping the nourishing broth.

"How long has it been since you've eaten?" Gil asked.

"Almost a week. Ran out of everything I could eat." Donny slurped down more soup. "Didn't even have a single bone left to give Blu."

Gil glanced toward the husky. "When Blu showed up, I knew something wasn't right." Fed and warm, the big dog lay on a pallet at the foot of his master's bed. The canine had done his job and had earned the right to rest. Furry body heaving, he emitted a light snore.

"Settin' Blu free was the only thing I knew to do. At least one of us had a chance of makin' it."

"Didn't you know the storm was coming?"

"I did. But I couldn't get to town to get any extra supplies. My truck broke down and I haven't been able to get it runnin'."

Florene claimed the empty bowl. "Maybe it's time to think about getting a cell phone," she murmured, offering the hot tea. "I know service can be spotty, but it's better than nothing."

"Had one, but I had to give it up," Donny mumbled, dropping his gaze. "Things got a little short. Haven't worked in a few months, and I don't have much money." Snuffling, he wiped his nose with the back of his hand. "I was going to hike down to your place, Gil, but I got to feelin' poorly."

Gil couldn't help but wince with guilt. He knew his neighbor had problems, and no one to rely on. The tremors racking Donny's body indicated it wasn't just a simple virus. Sweating, fever and clammy skin were also signs something else was going on.

"When's the last time you had a drink?"

Donny snuffled again. "Ain't had a single drop in weeks." Tears suddenly welled up in his eyes. "I swear. I—I've been fightin' to quit 'cos I want to get sober." His hands trembled, betraying the battle within, a war against the demon gripping him for far too long.

"Aye. Glad to hear it."

"I've been tryin' to make some changes, be a better man." As he spoke, a spark of determination ignited within the sick man—a spark that said he wanted to live.

Florene stepped closer, resting a hand of encouragement on Donny's shoulder. "I think that's a brave thing to do."

"I've been tired of bein' alone." The loss had carved a space within his bereaved soul. "Hannah passed twenty years ago, you know. My daughter's gone, too. Haven't seen Mary in a long time. Don't even know my grandson, either. 'Cept for them, I got no family. Most everyone's died or moved away."

Gil's heart twisted. After Hannah Reese's unexpected passing, Donny's life had spiraled into a seemingly endless abyss of alcohol-fueled escapades. Donny could often be found slouched in front of the local tavern. His clothes, once neat and respectable, hung loosely on his gaunt frame, bearing the stains of countless drunken spills. Torn between pity and disdain, folks couldn't help but watch as the lost man stumbled through life, dragging his young daughter behind him. Though only in his early fifties, Donny looked much older than his actual age.

Witnessing the plight of a man who'd lost everything, a man haunted by the absence of the ones he held dearest, Gil felt the weight of regret press down hard. The unbearable burden threatened to consume him. What he saw in Donny Reese was something he feared would happen to him.

That he would end up alone.

"Having your *familie* closer would be something *gut* in your life. I'll pray *Gott* opens the door for that to happen."

"Would you do that for me?" Expression troubled, Donny searched for a connection that would offer solace. "Reach out to the Lord on my behalf?"

Gil didn't hesitate. The request was unexpected, but welcome. "I would be honored." His belief in *Gott* had been his strength throughout his entire life. He couldn't fathom living without knowing the Holy Spirit.

"Don't know much about prayin'," Donny added. "But I hope I can be forgiven for my bad ways."

Florene took a small step back, her hands clasped as if in nervousness. Her *kapp*, neatly secured around her face, framed eyes that reflected a mixture of uncertainty and longing.

Gil looked between the two. "*Gott* is a redeemer," he said, using the moment to teach and encourage. "The Lord has plucked many sinners from far more difficult circumstances than yours."

"I want to know my maker, but I've always been afraid of what He'd see in me. A no-good bum who always drank too much."

"It's easy to think you're not *gut* enough to be saved." An ache of longing touched Florene's whispery voice.

Making up his mind, Donny offered skeletal fingers. "I want to be."

Kneeling by the bed, Gil grasped the older man's frail hands. The best place for a believer to be when petitioning *Gott* was on his knees. It showed humility and respect.

"Dear Lord, I ask You to look upon this man with Thy mercy. Open his heart to Thy presence and reveal Thyself to him. Guide him through the shadows that darken his soul and lead him to the light of Thy love. Amen."

Donny closed his eyes, surrendering. "Thank you."

Gil rose. "You're welcome to come to church when you're feeling better."

"I doubt the bishop would want me around. I'm not Amish, and people still blame me for stealin' Hannah away."

"A lot of water has passed under the bridge and folks aren't as judging as they were years ago. Bishop Harrison welcomes anyone who wants to hear the Word. He always has."

"I might do that." A pause lingered before Donny's gaze shifted toward the bureau in the corner. "Would you be willing to do something else for me?"

"Ja."

"There's a letter to Mary, just there. I wrote it before I got to feelin' bad, but I never sent it."

Florene found the letter on the bureau and brought it back to the sick man's bedside. "Why not?"

"I was afraid what her answer would be." Donny's eyes glistened as he shared the painful truth: fear and pride had kept him from reaching out. Now, faced with the fragility of life, he yearned to make peace before his health entirely abandoned him. "I'd like her and Benjamin to come home, so I can make things right. I wasn't a good dad. But I want to be before my time runs out."

Gil nodded. "We'll take it to the post office as soon as we can get to town."

It was a promise he intended to keep.

Coat pulled tight and blanket tucked around her legs, Florene kept her eyes fixed on the road ahead as they headed home. A bracing zephyr wind nipped her cheeks, prodding her to raise her scarf to the level of her eyes. It was well past noon, and the landscape was bathed in soft, muted shadows. The air was crisp, the temperature having dropped close to unbearable. Gil sat beside her. The only sounds were the rhythmic crunch of the horse's hooves in the deep snow and the occasional jingle of its harness.

Though she was outwardly serene, her thoughts were all over the place. *The letter.* Tucked away in her basket, the weight of a sick man's request lingered in her mind—a father seeking reconciliation with his daughter.

Would it be right to mail it?

The facts as she knew them tumbled through her mind. Leaving Burr Oak, Mary Reese had fled the poverty of her childhood, finding sanctuary with a cousin on her mother's side. By the address on the letter, Mary lived in Beeville. The smaller Amish settlement was just an hour's drive from Corpus Christi. A peaceful town, it was the perfect place for the young woman to reconnect with the values her *mutter* had abandoned to marry an *Englischer*.

Gil shifted his weight, adjusting to a more comfortable position on the buggy's unpadded wooden seat. "You're awfully quiet," he ventured, breaking the lull.

"I was just thinking about Donny—the way he asked for you to pray for him."

"What about it?"

"Do you think he meant it, that he'll change his ways?"

"Why not? The Lord works in mysterious ways. He's taken more than one sinner and turned them into a vessel for His grace." Taking his gaze off the road, he glanced her way. Certainty was etched into the lines around his eyes. "Being sick and alone, Donny got a *gut* scare. Sometimes a man needs that to show him what's important."

"If he means to change, really change, I'm glad—"

"But?"

Florene's pulse quickened. Was Donny's desire for change genuine or a fleeting moment of remorse? "Is it right of him to try and drag Mary back to something she tried so hard to get away from?" she demanded, compassion warring with skepticism. "And what would she be bringing her *sohn* into? A piece of dirt in the middle of nowhere with junked cars in the yard."

"Those things mean nothing," Gil said, his staunch figure illuminated by the soft glow of the buggy's battery-powered running lights. "What does mean something is that Donny's trying to change. It's up to Mary to decide if she can forgive him."

She sighed, her breath visible in the chilly air. "Does he deserve it?"

"No one earns or deserves forgiveness. It's a privilege, not a right anyone can claim." His gaze met hers, his expression compassionate.

"So, you're saying Mary should let the past go?"

"I know what I'd do." Just as Gil answered, the

buggy hit a rough patch in the road, jostling their shoulders together. He slowed the horse, steadying the animal's eager pace toward home.

"Then you're going to mail the letter?"

"Gave my word, and I will. Once we let it go, the Lord can take over. If Mary's become a woman of faith, she'll know the right thing to do."

Despite his reply, Florene couldn't help but feel a weighty responsibility in delivering the missive of reconciliation.

Why does it bother me?

She couldn't quite grasp the answer. The pieces all seemed abstract and didn't fit together to form any sort of a clear picture. And maybe that was the answer. Looking ahead, tomorrow loomed ahead like a big, black hole. More than *something* was the fear that there would be...*nothing*.

The Kestler farm came into view, a welcome distraction from her troubling thoughts.

The buggy slowed its pace as they turned into the driveway, the creaking sound beneath the wooden wheels signaling the journey's end. Smoke curled from the chimney of the old *haus*, a promise of warmth and comfort waiting within.

Gil guided the buggy around to the back of the barn where a freestanding shed provided shelter and storage for the vehicle. Blowing out a loud snuffle, the mare came to a halt. "Glad to be home safe." He pulled the hand brake and hopped to the ground. "You go on inside. I'll get the horse un-hitched and put away."

Florene climbed down. It would take at least twenty minutes for him to undo all the straps and buckles and put the tack away before tending the horse. It wasn't fair to make him do the majority of the work. By splitting the chore, they could get things done faster. "I'll get the stall ready."

"You don't mind?"

"*Nein*. I'll pour out feed and fresh water, too."

"It would be a help," he allowed, swiping at his frostbitten nose. "This cold is about to get the better of me."

"I'll get it done." She offered a quick wave and hurried to the front of the barn. Pulling open one of the double doors, she slipped inside. Dust particles danced in the dim illumination, creating an ethereal atmosphere within the expansive space. Tools and other implements were neatly stacked, and the scent of manure and feed tickled her nostrils. The rhythmic sounds of livestock shifting in their stalls and the clucking of chickens filled the air.

She paused, giving the rabbit pen a check. Noses twitching, the rabbits poked their heads out of their hutches, hoping she'd bought a treat.

"I'll bring some scraps later," she called out with a smile.

Amid the animal noises, she detected a human

voice—an almost imperceptible murmur that seemed out of place.

Florene cocked her head. No, she hadn't imagined it. It was the unmistakable voice of a man, resonating from the tack room.

Eli? It wasn't unusual for him to be out there. Equipment for the horses was stored there, along with other supplies. He was probably tending a chore, most likely some leather tack needing repair.

Might as well let him know they were home.

Approaching the half-open door, she peeked inside. The sight that greeted her was far from the ordinary. Eli stood in the dimly lit room, back turned toward her, holding a small, illuminated rectangle pressed to the side of his head.

Florene took a quick step away, hoping he hadn't noticed her. Heart pounding, she couldn't help but overhear what he was saying.

"Ja," he confirmed. "I'm working on the details now."

Unwilling to leave, she stood, frozen in place. Eli wasn't doing anything wrong. The *Ordnung* allowed for the use of electronic devices like smartphones for business or emergency purposes. Still, Eli had never indicated he owned one.

A man who sneaks around and hides isn't honest.

Determined to find out more, she leaned in closer. As far as she could tell, the speaker on the other end of the line seemed persistent. In response, Eli kept running a hand through his hair and nodding as he listened.

"Yes, sir. I'm looking forward to it," he replied to the caller. "As soon as I can get to town, I'll take care of it. After that, I'll be free to proceed." A pause to listen and then a little more. "Uh, huh. *Ja*. I promise, there'll be no backing out. I've made up my mind about what's best for my *familie*. I'm ready to make the change."

Sensing the conversation was close to its end, she backed away from the door. Startled by the stamping of a horse, one of the barn cats darted across her path. Tripping over the feline, she let out a loud gasp,

"*Ach*, no!" As her arms flailed in desperate search of stability, her ankle twisted beneath her weight. A hot spike shot up her leg. Tail flicking, the cat darted away.

The door to the tack room flew open.

"What are you doing there?" Eli threw out the words in a growl.

Tears welled in Florene's eyes as the ache pulsed through her ankle. "I—I heard a noise," she stammered, voice trembling.

A tense silence hung between them as each looked at the other. The barn, once a sanctuary, now felt charged with tension.

Eli moved with predatory determination, closing the distance between them. Lunging out, he grabbed her arm, tugging her close. "I asked what you were doing," he demanded through clenched teeth.

Florene cringed, fearful of what he might do. The past momentarily collided with the present, triggering haunting memories of the abuse she'd endured in past times. Zane's face suddenly flashed through her mind—the hate in his gaze, the pain of his open palm striking hard and fast. Eli looked just as angry—and just as willing to do her harm.

"I don't know!" she flung back as the barn transformed into a chaotic scene. Sensing disharmony, the livestock began to react. The animals immediately picked up on the disturbance. The horses shifted and stamped in their stalls, as did the cows and goats.

Mistaking her babbling for defiance, Eli leaned in with a menacing glare. "Whatever you think you heard, you didn't." A dangerous edge laced his tone. His grip tightened. And to back up his threat, he gave her a vicious shake. "You better keep your mouth shut, or there'll be consequences."

Desperate to escape harm, Florene jerked out of his grasp. "You're hurting me!" she cried, stumbling away from his reach. A ragged sob pressed past her lips as pain surged up her leg.

Ignoring her distress, he waved a menacing fist. "Swear on your faith you won't say a word."

Florene's eyes darted to the pitchfork leaning against the wooden stall. Instincts kicking in, she grabbed the tool with determination. Her fingers closed around the rough wooden handle, holding it like a makeshift weapon.

"I won't be threatened—not by you or anyone else!" Fueled by fear, she was determined to fight back with every ounce of her strength.

Eli's eyes widened as he realized the tables were turning. Sensing the danger, he wisely took a step back, raising his hands in a gesture of surrender. "I'm just saying it's nothing that concerns you," he said, trying to smooth over his ugly outburst. He even smiled a little, attempting to slip back behind an affable facade.

She kept the pitchfork firmly in place. His temper and fear of discovery made him a dangerous enemy. And the glint of malice never left his gaze. "That's all you had to say."

"Then I'm saying so, and you'd better remember it." Turning on his heel, Eli strode toward the door. Pausing, he added a final warning. "Just as soon as the weather clears, you find a way to be gone. You don't belong here, *Englisch*." He threw out the last word as it was intended to be, a slur. His veiled threats lingered as he disappeared.

A long minute passed. And then another.

Just like that, it was over.

Exhaling a breath she hadn't realized she was holding, Florene slowly lowered the pitchfork that had become her lifeline. The surging adrenaline that had propelled her into desperate self-defense began to ebb, making room for a potent sense of relief. In that moment of vulnerability, she had unearthed a reservoir of inner strength, and the taste of empowerment lingered in the air.

I won't be manhandled ever again.

However, the dissipating tension didn't signify the end of her entanglement in Eli's secrets. The uncertain aftermath still crackled in the air. People only got angry when they were caught doing something they shouldn't.

A fresh surge of uneasiness raced through her veins, each heartbeat echoing the suspicion that Eli was up to no good. The pulse in her temples quickened even as the question loomed, demanding an answer.

What is Eli hiding?

Chapter Ten

The rest of the day passed as it should.

Later, everyone gathered around the roaring fire, seeking solace from the cold as the bitter afternoon descended into night. Crackling flames danced, casting out a golden glow of warmth and comfort. Supper was served early, a hearty pot of meaty chili with a side of fresh, buttered cornbread. Conversation rose and fell, touching on this and that.

Fussing over a stitch she'd dropped, Almeda lowered her knitting. "Don't know what's wrong with my fingers. I just can't get this right today."

Florene looked up from her book and attempted a reassuring smile. "Knitting always eluded me. I never could do it." Shifting her foot to a more comfortable position, she winced.

Cradling a mug of *kaffee*, Gil gave her an anxious look. "Still giving you a twinge?"

Oh, dear. She'd hoped that subject wouldn't come up again. Entering the barn not five minutes after Eli departed, he was unaware a scuffle had taken place. There was no reason to say anything. It would just make trouble. And that was something she didn't need any more of.

"*Nein*. It's fine." A glance toward Eli affirmed she'd said the right thing. Since their encounter in the barn, he'd lurked close, never out of earshot. Lips pressed tight, he shot a narrow look of warning her way.

"I feel bad you got hurt doing something I should have been taking care of," Gil said.

She forced a laugh, hoping it didn't sound fake. "I just tripped over a cat, is all."

Guilt creased the big man's face. "It was my job."

"Please, don't feel bad," she said reassuringly. "I wanted to help."

"*Ach*, animals can be pesky," Almeda said, showing her own bandaged foot. "Look what happened to me, milking that ornery old cow."

"I've always worried about that," Nella repeated for the hundredth time. "That someone would get hurt and we'd be too far out in the country to get help. People can get seriously injured—or even die. Why, just look at what happened to poor old Donny Reese, all sick and alone. He could've perished."

"Donny's fine," Gil explained patiently. "We left plenty of food, and I'll be checking on him."

Tucking Isaiah's blanket around his tiny body, Nella refused to be deterred. "What if Isaiah gets hurt?" she demanded. "What would we do?"

Eli cleared his throat, breaking his stillness. "I don't like being out so far now that I've got a *youngie*. I'm beginning to believe living in town would be better for us."

"You've lived here all your life," Almeda countered. "And done just fine."

"No one ever takes my concerns seriously," Nella pouted. "It's like everything I say goes in one ear and out the other."

"I'm listening," Eli said. "And I'm doing my best."

"Well, it's not *gut* enough!" Nella snapped back. "*Daed* says a man should provide for his *familie*. You promised me better when you were courting me, and you've done nothing at all!"

Almeda bristled. "Eli provides. You've never gone without."

"But everything is so old and out of date," Nella whined. "It's like taking a step back a hundred years. We might be Amish, but we're allowed to enjoy better, just like anyone else."

"I've never known anyone so discontent," Almeda said.

"I want to live in town, closer to my *mamm*." Turning on her *ehmann*, she pounced. "Eli, you promised we would!"

Almeda gave her youngest a long look. "Is that true?"

Called out, Eli floundered. "Well, um…"

Embarrassed to be caught in the middle of the

argument, Florene attempted to rise. A few hours ago, Eli had made himself clear. She didn't belong, and he wanted her gone.

"I'll give you all your privacy." Thankfully, her twisted ankle held her weight, giving her the confidence to take a few steps forward.

"It's nothing we haven't talked about before," Almeda said, waving her back. "And if it isn't for everyone's ears, then nobody should say it."

"If you say so." Looking back into her past, it wasn't hard to recall how her *familie* ranch struggled in past times. She was fully aware that work outside of farming had become increasingly necessary because of economic changes. Many non-farming Amish labored within their communities, serving traditional needs such as the repair of farm and household equipment and operating horse-and-buggy trades. Others had begun to take *Englisch* jobs to keep food on the table.

"Is that something you want to do?" Gil asked. "Move to town?"

"I'd like to do better, see some easier times," Eli confirmed.

Dismay etched Almeda's brow. "You would leave the homestead?"

"It's nothing we should have to suffer," Nella insisted.

Almeda's frustration bubbled to the surface. "Oh, Nella—you're not suffering. You're just selfish!"

Confronted with the truth, Nella immediately burst into tears. "No one understands!" she bawled.

Eli leaned in. "Now, *liebling*, don't cry."

Nella backed him off with a glare. "Don't you try and sweet-talk me! You promised me you'd be able to do better. But all you do is scrape the ground and bring up nothing. Well, I have had enough!" Scooping up Isaiah, she fled upstairs. A few seconds later, the heavy slam of her bedroom door was heard below.

A moment of shocked silence followed.

"That girl," Almeda finally said, shaking her head. "She wasn't made for farm life."

Eli made no effort to follow his wife. "I think she's planning to leave me," he murmured in a low voice.

"She wouldn't…"

"*Ja.* I think she would." Frustrated, Eli ran his hands through his hair. "If things don't get settled soon, I'm going to lose my *fraa*."

Mother and son locked eyes, a battle between tradition and progress. The flickering flames in the hearth cast dancing shadows on the generations torn between the past and an uncertain future.

Looking between them, Gil stepped in. "It isn't anything that's going to happen today," he said, attempting to ease the tension.

"Suppose you're right." His mother sighed, weariness etched on her face. "But I guess changes are going to be coming, whether we like them or not."

"I'm only doing what *Gott* says is right," Eli said. "Genesis says a man must leave his *vater* and *mutter* and hold fast to his *fraa*. I'll do what's best for my *familie*."

Amid the exchange, Florene held her tongue. A profound wave of sorrow engulfed her. Powerless to speak out, all she could do was watch helplessly as the tumultuous drama unfolded, shredding the fabric of familial peace and harmony. Once again, the gravity of the situation had fallen squarely on Almeda's frail shoulders.

"My mind needs a little peace." With a deliberate motion, she reached for her cane and pushed herself up. "Think I'll go to bed." Quiet determination filled her eyes, reflecting a lifetime of resilience. With each measured step of hers, the cane became an extension of her willpower, supporting her as she moved through the living room. The wooden floor creaked beneath her, echoing the struggle in her aged bones.

That left three. Silence lingered. The old windup clock above the mantel struck nine, indicating the hour was growing late.

Florene glanced at the book in her lap. The responsibilities of the coming day tugged at her conscience, reminding her of the chores that awaited. Still, an unspoken sense of unease kept her anchored to the chair. "Think I'll read another chapter."

Gil gave a curious look. "What are you reading?"

"*Gulliver's Travels*," she said, tilting the pages for him to see.

Eli glanced toward the shelf she'd taken it from. "*Mamm* bought those books back in the days when they sold encyclopedias through the mail. She was tickled the set included a dozen classic novels, too."

Unwilling to be engaged, but unable to ignore him, Florene offered a wry smile. "We had the same set, I believe. Back then, we used them for school." Published decades ago, the encyclopedias were badly out of date. Still, a good story was timeless.

"I copied tons of stuff out of them for class," Eli admitted. "Now all kids have to do is look it up on the internet."

"I did the same. We all did, pretty much."

"What's the book about?" Gil asked.

"It's about a man named Gulliver, a surgeon and sea captain, who visits remote regions of the world, and it describes his adventures." Since beginning their lessons, she'd discovered a desire to increase her knowledge, too.

"Sounds like something I'd like." Giving a serious nod, he added. "I'm going to read it someday."

Eli snorted with derision. "Oh, please… You

can barely make it through the first-grade primers as it is." Waving his hands, he began to speak in a derogatory manner. "*See the dog run* is about all you can manage."

Gil refused to be cowed. "I'm going to learn more. I might be slow, but I will."

Florene looked between the two brothers. Aside from a familial resemblance, they were nothing alike. "I think it's admirable," she countered. "Just because we leave school doesn't mean we quit learning. No one's born knowing everything."

"Suppose that's so," Eli conceded. "I'm not saying he's incapable of learning, either. It's just that he was the one who got himself kicked out of school."

As Gil's gaze locked onto his brother, the air in the room thickened with tension. "Eli, please don't."

"What?" Eli retorted. "Don't tell the truth?"

A knot tightened in Florene's stomach. She knew Gil didn't have a chance to go to school, but no one had ever said why. What could be so terrible?

"It's okay if you don't want to talk about it," she said. Eli's relentless criticism of Gil bothered her deeply.

Gil fidgeted nervously. "It happened a long time ago. No reason to bring it up now." His expression betrayed a mixture of embarrassment and shame.

"It wasn't Gil's fault," Eli suddenly blurted. "He didn't mean to hurt that boy. He's always been big, and he didn't know how to control his strength."

It was a day etched into the fabric of his being—the day everything changed. Memories of the incident still haunted him.

Swallowing hard, Gil stared into the depths of his empty cup. Decades had passed since that day. Thankfully, most folks had forgotten and moved on.

He had not. He never would. Not as long as he lived.

He cast a glance toward his brother. "Why'd you have to say that?"

"Just talking. It happened. No use denying it." Oblivious to the hurt he'd inflicted, Eli turned to address Florene directly. "I know you must have wondered why he never finished school."

She returned a tight smile. "It wasn't any of my business."

"I thought you should know," Eli said, spreading his hands in all innocence. "Gil's got a temper. Matter of fact, it's gotten away from him a time or two."

A flicker of concern touched her expression. She quickly erased it. "We all have our moments," she said, speaking in a low, calm tone. "Maybe we should discuss things we've done ourselves before pointing fingers at others. Hypocrisy always trips us up, wouldn't you agree?" Aimed directly, her reply flew like a sharp arrow.

The color drained from Eli's face. A flicker of anger danced in his eyes, belying the confident mask he usually wore. It was as if Florene had pulled back the curtain on a carefully staged performance, revealing a tangled web beneath.

Gil looked between the two of them. Something seemed to be simmering between them. He just didn't know what it was.

Uneasy, Eli glanced toward the clock on the mantel. "I believe my *fraa*'s waited long enough for me." Rising to his feet, he yawned and stretched. "I'm going to bed."

Florene offered a nod. "Then I'll bid you *gute nacht.*"

"Same to you."

Gil breathed a sigh of relief. Put in his place, Eli had run off with his tail tucked between his legs. He couldn't say he minded. Not one bit.

"That was uncomfortable," Florene commented, breaking the tension.

"*Ja*, it was."

"I don't know how you stand it. Eli's always on you for something."

"He's always been that way." He shrugged. "Guess I'm used to it by now."

"You should stand up for yourself," she blurted. "Stop acting like Mr. Nice Guy."

Unable to look her in the eyes, Gil glanced into his empty cup. "*Nein*. Just leave it be."

She leaned forward. "Why won't you fight back?"

He refused to look up. "Because of what I did."

She made a scoffing sound. "Was it really that bad? Or is Eli just making it sound that way?"

Hands gripping the ceramic mug, Gil took a deep breath. "I'd rather not say." His words were low, barely mumbled. Even as he spoke, a painful torrent of regret and shame came flooding back.

"Keeping things to yourself never helps," she said softly, her voice tinged with a quiet sorrow.

"I'm the one who has to deal with it." Shaking his head, he rose. "It's getting late. I should go." He strode into the kitchen and paused at the back door to reach for his hat and coat.

Laying her book aside, Florene followed. "Running off won't make it go away," she warned, placing her hands on her hips. "It'll only fester, and then you'll feel worse inside."

Gil hesitated. She was right. Being sorry had never made his remorse go away, either. "No, I guess it won't."

As she gazed up at him, her eyes expressed a readiness to hear what he had to say. "I'm willing to listen if you need someone to talk to." She nodded toward the kitchen table. "I'll freshen the *kaffee* and we'll talk."

Releasing a sigh, he returned his hat and coat

to their place. He wasn't sure what he was going to say. But he'd agreed to stay, and he would.

He sat, waiting for Florene to join him. She emptied the dregs out of the percolator and rinsed it out before adding a measure of fresh grounds. Setting the pot on the stove to perk, she retrieved the cups they'd abandoned in the living room. Washing and drying both, she set them on the counter in preparation to receive the hot, steaming brew. Comfortable in her role as caretaker, she moved with practiced ease.

"Here you go," she said, delivering two full cups a few minutes later. To make the visit more hospitable, she served the *kaffee* with oatmeal cookies arranged attractively on a plate.

"Danke," Gil said, accepting his cup.

She sat across from him. "This is much more comfortable, don't you think?" she asked, adding sugar and a splash of milk to hers.

"Ja."

"You want to tell me what happened?"

Gil hesitated. If he closed his eyes, he could easily picture the schoolhouse in his childhood, where his innocence had given way to regret.

"I guess I should start at the beginning. Before Eli was born, I had a sister."

Surprise lifted her brows. "I didn't know."

"Annabella. We were close, born just over a year apart from each other. I was the big one.

And she was the little one, being born sick and all. Down syndrome is what the doctors called it."

Her expression turned sympathetic. "I'm sorry to hear that."

Memories of a laughing sprite with big brown eyes flashed across his mind's screen. "Annabella was never strong, but she was feisty. When she learned to walk, she was kind of my little shadow. Everything I did, she wanted to do, too." An unexpected rush of emotion closed his throat. His younger sister had been a ray of happiness, and he'd adored her.

Reaching out, Florene covered his hand with hers. Her quiet presence offered solace. "I think I'd understand if you don't want to go on."

Struggling to keep his composure, Gil prepared to confront the ghosts of his past. "*Nee*, I want to." Having kept silent for more than twenty years, he felt the need to keep going. "Everything was fine until Annabella got old enough to go to school. She looked different, and the other *youngies* didn't understand."

Florene nodded. "When I was in school, we had a few special needs students like that. We were taught they were '*life's sunbeams*' and to treat them like everyone else. They had a teacher who'd gone to an *Englisch* college to learn how to instruct them."

"Most everyone accepted Annabella. But there was this one fella, Jimmy Allgyr. He did things like throw rocks at stray dogs and pinch the girls until they'd cry. I didn't like him, not one bit."

A frown of disapproval crossed her face. "There always has to be a bully."

Gil took a sip of *kaffee* to distract himself from the ache. "*Ja.* The ugly things he said made Annabella cry," he said after lowering his cup. "Seeing her like that made me mad. It wasn't her fault she was that way, different and such. One day, things got out of hand, and I couldn't take it anymore."

"You got in a fight?"

Nodding, he stared past her, unable to look her in the eyes. He vividly recalled every detail etched deep in his memory. At the time, it had seemed like an ordinary scuffle, just boys being boys. But it wasn't. Anger turning into a tempest, he'd acted out in rage.

"I hurt Jimmy," he said, determined to speak honestly. "He took Annabella's pencil and broke it, just to be mean. I saw him do it and jumped up. Gave him a shove, just to show him how it felt to be picked on. Jimmy stumbled and fell…and hit his head on the edge of a desk." As he spoke, the heavy weight of remorse descended all over again. In that moment he wasn't a grown man, but a seven-year-old boy struck with the realization that he'd done something terrible. He remembered looking at his schoolmate crumpled on the floor. It had happened so fast that he hadn't stopped to think about the consequences.

Florene's eyes widened as she grasped the gravity of his confession. "Oh, Gil. I know you didn't mean to hurt him."

Gil sucked in a painful breath. "I thought I was protecting Annabella, but instead, I hurt another person."

"Was Jimmy all right?"

"He was okay, but it upset a lot of people." The fight, though brief, had left an indelible mark on him. The realization of the pain he had inflicted upon a fellow member of their tight-knit community had settled on his shoulders like a heavy shroud. He was bigger than Jimmy, and stronger, too. Anger clashing with upset, his innocence had collided with a darker force.

"But why? You were only protecting your sister."

Gil felt a tightness in his chest. Following the incident, the church elders had convened in a solemn meeting to discuss the severity of his actions and contemplate an appropriate response. A decision was reached: he would be taken out of school. This consequence, though painful, was deemed necessary because of his size. He was just so much stronger than the other children, even those twice his age. The expulsion felt like an exile from the community that had always been his haven.

"People always treated me differently because I'm so big." He swallowed hard, his throat dry.

"Because of what I did—raising a hand against another—I couldn't go back to school. To keep the peace, *Daed* agreed. He told me not to worry about reading or writing. Put me right to work, learning to train horses. That's what I've done ever since."

"It still doesn't sound fair to me. Jimmy should have been called out, too, for his bad behavior."

"It was fair to the others." Regret and shame lashed him. "I've tried to do right since then. I made a promise to *Gott* I'd never raise a hand toward anyone or anything." Nodding resolutely, he turned his palms up. "And I meant it. To this day, I've never done it again."

"I believe you." Her soft voice resonated like a hymn, offering solace to his troubled soul. Her support conveyed a silent assurance, encouraging him to go on.

"I wish I could tell you that was the end of trouble. But a year later, Annabella left this world. Her heart wasn't strong."

"I'm so sorry."

"*Mamm* and *Daed* never talked about her after she passed." Sadness clutched his throat all over again. "*Mamm*'s got her things packed away, but she never looks at them anymore. She was so happy when Eli was born. It's like Annabella never existed. I feel bad because it seems like I'm the only one who remembers her. I don't want to hurt *Mamm*, so I don't say anything."

Florene sadly brushed away a tear. "I'm sorry for your loss."

"*Gott* says not to mourn those who have passed. I believe Annabella found peace with the Lord."

"It doesn't stop the pain of losing someone you love."

No, it didn't. But he had no chance to say it. The clock above the mantel sang out—releasing eleven long chimes.

"Didn't realize it was so late." The wooden chair scraped against creaky floorboards when he pushed away from the table. "I should get on home."

Florene unexpectedly caught his hand. "I just want to tell you that you're a *gut mann*, Gilead. Remember that. Always."

Their gazes met in an unspoken understanding—a bond transcending the mistakes of the past.

The tension knotting Gil's shoulders unraveled, replaced by a sense of relief he hadn't known in years. In that fleeting moment, he was convinced *Gott* above had extended forgiveness to him. It wasn't a thunderous revelation but a gentle, subtle understanding that settled in his heart.

Letting go of the past, he could finally look toward the promise of a brighter tomorrow.

Chapter Eleven

"You sure you want your hair cut that short?"

Gil took a deep breath and nodded. "*Ja*. Cut it all off." A testament to years of neglect and indifference to his appearance, his long, unruly hair hung down to his shoulders. He'd spent years not caring about his appearance, but today was different. Rising well before the sun, he'd headed over to catch *Mamm* before she started breakfast. He was ready to make a change, and that would be the best time.

Mamm chuckled, mirth crinkling her eyes. "Then that's what I'll do." Bidding him to sit in a chair near the sink, she draped an old towel around his shoulders.

Stomach fluttering with nerves, Gil sat. "I know it's been a long time coming," he said, lacing his fingers before settling his hands in his lap.

"Glad you've decided to make some changes." Humming a lively tune, *Mamm* combed through his overgrown locks, unsnarling the tangles. "Always did look like a rat's nest anyway. Don't know how you tolerated it." Satisfied she had everything right, she set her scissors to work.

Gil winced as the first strands fell to the floor. For years, he'd used his messy appearance as a shield, a way to keep people at arm's length. Having done some praying and hard thinking, he'd decided he wanted better. Not only for himself but for the future he hoped to build. A future as an educated man, who could read and talk properly without people laughing and pointing behind his back.

Mamm kept snipping. After the last strands of unruly hair tumbled down, she stepped back to survey her handiwork. "Done."

He cautiously touched his hair, feeling the strange sensation of freedom on his neck. "Does it look okay?" As was the custom, most Amish men wore their hair in a way that didn't draw attention to the individual. The most common look was a tapered scissor cut, leaving enough length to neatly blend the layers.

Whisking the towel off his shoulders, *Mamm* brushed the stray hairs into the nearby trash bin. "See for yourself."

Gil hesitated before standing up. He didn't have a mirror handy, but the windowpane above the sink would do. As he gazed into the glass, his eyes widened in astonishment. "Well, I'll be," he muttered, genuinely surprised. The short style enhanced and sharpened his features in a complimentary way. His once wild and untamed appearance was replaced by a more polished version.

"Sometimes, we need a change to see ourselves differently." *Mamm*'s gaze grew soft as she put away the scissors and comb. "I forgot how much you looked like your *daed*."

Gil rubbed a hand against his smooth cheek. He'd cleaned up before coming over and his face lacked its usual layer of whiskers. "Do I?"

"Ja," she said, smiling at the memory. "The spitting image."

Gil glanced at his reflection again. As he did, memories flooded back, painting vivid images of Silas Kestler. A figure of quiet dignity, the older man had worked the fields with a steady determination. His father's broad shoulders bore the weight of responsibility without complaint. After a hard day of labor, *Daed*'s laughter echoed through the *haus*, lifting the spirits of everyone around him. His wisdom, the way he spoke of the land as a gift from *Gott*. More than a past now gone, it was a time when a man's simplest gestures carried the weight of a thousand promises.

"I miss him, every day."

Tears welled up in *Mamm*'s eyes. Her ache was palpable, grief an uninvited guest that lingered in every corner of her heart. "Me, too," she said softly. "But I can't help but be proud when I see you standing there."

He guffawed softly. "Never thought you were."

"I am," *Mamm* said, offering a watery smile. "I always have been. I'm glad you're taking better care of yourself."

"Never felt like it mattered." Sweeping his fingers through his short hair, he marveled at the absence of snarled tangles. It was a foreign sensation, strangely liberating. For the first time, he was willing to acknowledge and appreciate the gifts *Gott* had given him. He wasn't the ogre he'd always believed himself to be. Now, his broad shoulders and big hands felt like they fit.

A newfound sense of excitement filled him, spurred by the prospects of the days ahead. Suddenly there were places he wanted to go, and things he wanted to do.

The back door unexpectedly swung open. Bundled in heavy clothes, Eli stepped inside, stamping the snow off his boots. His breath formed tiny clouds in the air as he closed the door behind him.

"Just got back from the highway and—" As he caught sight of Gil, his jaw fell slack. *"Bruder?"* His brows rose high, curiosity tangling with disbelief. "Is that you?"

Gil nodded. *"Ja."*

Eli took off his hat and scarf. "You look—" he sized Gil up in a way that suggested a shift in their dynamic "—different."

"Better, I hope," Gil replied, unsure where his brother's sudden rigidity had come from. Right then and there, the spark of rivalry ignited between them all over again. He hadn't meant for it to. It just did.

"Can't believe it," Eli said, tugging off his gloves before stuffing them into his coat pockets. "You look like a decent human. Not half as ugly as I thought you were."

Gil let the insult pass. "No harm in cleaning up."

Unbuttoning his coat, Eli snagged it on a peg by the door. His scarf and hat followed. "I don't guess there is."

"Didn't know you were up so early," *Mamm* commented, pouring herself a fresh cup of *kaffee*. "Where've you been?"

Eli jerked a thumb over one shoulder. "Last night when I was listening to the radio, the news said the snowplows would be coming through. Thought I'd go down to the highway and look."

"They make it?"

"*Ja*. The big trucks are moving. I saw a couple of eighteen-wheelers go by."

A collective sigh of relief swept through the kitchen. Having vented its fury, the storm had finally moved on. Isolated close to two weeks, the farm had been cut off from the outside world. The welcome news brought a glimmer of relief. At last, there was a promise to escape the isolation that had held them captive. Freedom beckoned to those eager to make a trip into town for supplies and a bit of socializing.

"Glad the worst of it is over," *Mamm* declared. "I was starting to get a touch of cabin fever."

Eli headed toward the stove to warm his hands. "Me, too. Been needing to get into Burr Oak to take care of some business." The easy calm of the morning evaporated.

Mamm's expression tightened. "You and Nella still thinking about moving to town?"

"It's a consideration," Eli said, rubbing his hands together.

"Life isn't just about having better things. It's about roots, a place to belong. If you leave, what happens to your *sohn*'s connection to this land?"

"*Mamm*, you know my heart is in this farm," Eli replied, frustration etching his features. "But every season, we struggle more and more. I can't keep pouring sweat into this land when we're barely making ends meet."

"We've gone through hard times before. When the crops fail, we've got the horses to carry—"

Hand slicing the air, Eli cut her off. "That's my point, exactly! I don't want to have to rely on someone else when all the work I do in those fields comes to nothing." A mix of bitterness and jealously tinged his voice.

"I've never minded," Gil said. "Because that's what we're supposed to do. Take care of each other."

"Gil's right. If we stand together and have faith

in *Gott*, we'll pull through," *Mamm* said, her eyes pleading.

Eli shook his head. "Why don't you hear what I'm saying?" he demanded, turning sharply on his mother. "I want more. For me. For Nella. And, most of all, for Isaiah."

The outburst was a shock, a verbal slap in the face. The tension filling the kitchen thickened.

Mamm took a step closer to her youngest. "Do you realize what you're saying?"

Eli crossed his arms. "*Ja.* I do. I'm tired of asking you to settle things between Gil and me. If you won't decide, I will."

Spoiled since birth, Gil's younger brother expected to get what he wanted, *when* he wanted it. And he didn't much care how he achieved it. He'd wheedle and whine until things went his way. The desire for more had become an obsession.

"Don't give me that look, Gil," Eli snorted back. "You want things settled as much as I do."

Refusing to be baited, Gil shook his head. "Just let it be, Eli. *Daed* hasn't been in the grave a year."

"*Boi*s, please—" *Mamm* held up a hand, signaling for peace. "Turning on each other won't help anything."

Eli refused to heed. "A man's got the right to take matters into his own hands."

Mamm's expression pleaded for reconsideration. "Eli, don't—"

Simmering with impatience, Eli slammed his hand on the table. "Things need to be put down on paper—the legal and proper way."

Gil stepped up to his brother, using his size as a barrier. "Your temper's getting out of hand," he warned. "You'll mind how you talk to our *mutter*."

Eli sensibly backed off. *"Es tut mir leid,"* he said by way of an apology. Taking a seat at the table, he pressed his head into his hands. "I just want to take care of my *familie*." His voice trembled with just the right note of despair.

Unwilling to see her youngest in distress, *Mamm* moved to comfort him. "You're right," she murmured, setting a hand on his shoulder. "It all needs to be settled."

Eli raised his head, rubbing his hands up and down his bearded face as if exhausted.

"Soon?"

Mamm momentarily pressed her lips together. Deep lines of distress etched her eyes and mouth, making her appear much older than her actual age.

"Ja." She nodded.

And that was that.

In the silence that followed, the crackle of flames in the old woodstove provided a soundtrack to the emotional turmoil filling the kitchen. The air was heavy with the weight of conflicting desires and generational expectations.

Witnessing the last of the exchange, Gil felt

dismay grip his insides. Though he had no proof, suspicion pressed hard. He couldn't help but believe that Eli's actions were a veiled attempt to mislead. Echoing with the legacy of generations, the land seemed destined to fall prey to his younger brother's ambitions.

Lord, please let me be wrong, he silently prayed.

"You're awfully quiet. Is everything okay?"

Gaze fixed on the scenery as the buggy rolled down the streets, Florene shook her head. "I can't believe how much everything's changed. It's not like I remembered." Three years was a long time to be away.

"It's grown quite a bit," Gil said.

"Ja," she agreed, shifting in her seat. "Looks that way."

Everything she once knew seemed to have turned into a faraway echo. Burr Oak had grown, and new neighborhoods had consumed formerly empty lots. Eager to serve a growing population, a plethora of businesses lined the streets. Passing the storefronts, she saw faces she didn't recognize. The old blacksmith shop was now a bustling grocery store. The changes were undeniable, a testament to the passage of time. No longer trapped in tradition, the sleepy little village hummed with newfound energy. The clip-clop of horse hooves was drowned out by the constant drumbeat of progress.

"We got a new post office." Gil tapped his chest, a reminder of the letter tucked inside his coat. "And a hospital, too. Took *Mamm* there when she got hurt. Been a real blessing to have it. Don't have to go all the way to Eastland for emergencies now."

"I imagine." All she could do was try to take it all in. The community she'd remembered seemed like a distant dream.

Now that the weather had cleared, people seemed determined to be out and about. No longer a pristine white blanket, the snow had turned to slush, creating a miserable mess. Sidewalks had been shoveled and salted, but that didn't make walking much easier. Horses and wagons struggled to hold their own against the charge of gas-powered vehicles. Traffic snarled to a stop when the two modes of transportation collided.

The buggy rolled on, passing a liquor store and a bail bonds establishment. Located near traditional businesses offering Amish goods and services, such places stood out like a sore thumb.

Sitting in the rear passenger seat, Eli leaned forward. "Not all the changes are for the better," he declared, putting in his two cents' worth. "More *Englisch* coming in. They bring their trouble, and no one wants that."

Florene offered a thin smile, pretty sure she was part of the trouble he spoke about. "So I've heard."

"I tolerate them," Nella chimed in. "But that's about all." She sat by Eli, bundled in a heavy coat, a blanket covering her lap. To keep him safe, his parents had tucked Isaiah in a car seat near Nella's feet.

The buggy's wheels turned with a steady determination. The horse's harness jingled softly, blending with the sound of wooden wheels rolling over cobblestoned streets. It was like gliding through the present while being tethered to the past.

Tugging the reins, Gil guided the vehicle to a halt. "Here we are." A modest structure made of red bricks, the library was the first stop of the day. Its peaked roof, adorned with copper-colored shingles, added a touch of nostalgia to the landscape. A slightly weathered but lovingly maintained white fence encircled the grounds. The entrance gate, bearing a handcrafted wooden sign that read Burr Oak Public Library, creaked softly in the chilly breeze. A winding stone path led visitors to the entrance.

"Now, here's a place I never thought I'd see you walk into," Eli cracked.

"Don't tease," Almeda fussed, swatting a hand toward her younger *sohn.* "You should be proud your *bruder* is wanting to better himself."

Gil nodded. "I'm going to get a card so I can check books out."

"Don't know why you'd need one when you can't read," Eli mocked.

"I'm getting audiobooks," Gil corrected. "I'll be able to listen and learn more."

Eli sobered. "I guess that makes sense."

"Some people like them better than paper books," Nella added helpfully. "They used to have a large collection on cassette and CD."

"That's what I remember," Florene said. "I hope they haven't phased them out for digital options."

"Guess we'll find out." Gil set the hand brake and jumped down. The mare whinnied, snorting and tossing her mane.

Eli hopped to the front of the buggy, claiming the seat his brother had vacated. "You two can hang around while we get on with our errands."

"We'll be here." Walking around, Gil extended a hand. "May I help you down?"

Florene hesitated, her gaze lingering on his tidy appearance. Underneath his coat, he wore a white shirt, trousers held up by suspenders, and laced black boots. A broad-brimmed hat on his freshly cut hair cast a shadow over his clean-shaven face. Spiffed up, he looked like an entirely different man—one she found herself drawn to in a way she'd never anticipated.

Heart fluttering, she accepted his help. As her hand slid into his, a strange yet exhilarating warmth filled her. Every stolen glance, every fleeting touch, carried the weight of a thousand unspoken words. Though every fiber of her being longed to reciprocate, she knew deep down it was a path strewn with thorns. Allowing her emotions to rule her heart would be a mistake.

You can't, she warned herself. *It's not right*. Clashing with Eli had given her a wake-up call. He'd made it clear she wasn't welcome.

Descending to the ground, she subtly pulled her hand away. *"Danke."* She stepped onto the sidewalk and adjusted her scarf before pulling her coat tighter to fend off the biting cold. Changing her appearance had gone a long way toward helping her blend in. With a basket hooked over her arm, she looked like any Plain woman out on errands with her *familie*.

Coming out in public was her first step toward freedom. She couldn't hide forever. Confronting her fear of discovery was the only way forward. It wasn't a choice now, but a necessity.

"Nella wants to go to the craft store," Eli announced. "Then I'll take *Mamm* to do her business. After that, we'll come back to pick you up."

"How long are you going to be?" Gil asked.

"Don't know how long things will take. Depends on how long the lines are. We'll be back when we get back."

As they spoke, Almeda's frown deepened, clouding her usually serene expression with an uncharacteristic heaviness. Her shoulders slouched, and lines of worry etched her forehead.

She wasn't happy. But she wasn't saying anything, either. The air was thick, humming with tension.

"Fine, we're in no hurry," Gil said, waving them away.

Releasing the hand brake, Eli flicked the reins to urge the horse to get going. The buggy shuddered a little before rolling away. Rounding a nearby corner, it went out of sight.

Florene watched it go. The change in the older woman's demeanor was concerning. "Is something wrong?"

"*Mamm* and Eli had words early this morning before you and Nella got up."

"I'm sorry to hear that."

"Just some things they have to work out." Gil forced a smile that failed to reach his eyes. "Eli's been pushing to settle things with the farm."

"I see." Having lived in the household long enough to gather the details, she wasn't surprised. The strife in the Kestler family offered another reason she needed to move on. "You think she'll let him have it?"

Concern deepened the lines around Gil's eyes, shadowing his expression. "I don't know."

Florene crossed her arms, shivering a little as the breeze tugged her *kapp* with invisible fingers. "I'd be worried about anything Eli got his hands on."

"I pray *Mamm* does the right thing." Pushing out a breath, he drew back his shoulders and glanced toward their destination. "We'll go inside now. *Ja?*"

Proceeding side by side, they entered the building. Shelves lined with books, buzzing computers and people absorbed in their studies filled the vast space. Patrons, engrossed in their digital devices or absorbed in the pages of books, paid little attention to the newcomers. Now that technology had crept in, it wasn't unusual to see Plain folks texting on a cell phone or waiting to use one of the library computers. Although amendments in the *Ordnung* allowed their use, moderation was advised. Electronic devices were to be used as one would any tool, with care and caution.

Hat in hand, Gil looked lost. "Not sure I belong here," he whispered, afraid to speak louder. "Don't even know where to begin."

"Neither do I. Everything has changed so much."

Feeling overwhelmed, Florene approached the front desk, where a librarian was sorting through a stack of returned books. Clearing her throat, she spoke hesitantly, "Excuse me, ma'am, I'm afraid we're lost. Could you point us to the audiobooks?"

The librarian looked up, revealing a warm smile. Her hair was tied in a loose bun, and a pair of glasses perched on the bridge of her nose. *"Ja,"* she said, speaking in rough *Deitsch*. "Our multimedia section is quite extensive."

"Can you still check out a CD player, too?"

"You may select two audiobooks and a portable player for two weeks. Patrons must supply the batteries, however."

"*Gut.* My *freund* would like to get a library card."

Eyes gleaming with excitement, Gil nervously stepped up. "I reckon I've never had one before," he confessed, his rough hands fidgeting with the brim of his hat.

"There's a first time for everything." Laughing, the librarian produced an application and pen. "Fill this out and bring it back with your selections. I'll get it processed and show you how to use the player if you need help."

Gil's brow furrowed in uncertainty as his excitement seemed to falter for a moment.

Sensing his hesitation, Florene picked up the offerings. "It's just a formality. I'll help you."

Gratitude shone in his eyes. *"Danke."*

"You're welcome," the librarian said. "Let me know if you need help."

Leaving the circulation desk, they made their way to the audio section, where rows of CDs gleamed.

He eagerly scanned the shelves. "Do they have the Bible?"

"Of course." She guided him to the section where a variety of editions were neatly arranged. "This one has both the Old and New Testaments."

He carefully selected the box set, handling it with reverence. "This is the one I'd like to get."

"You can pick another."

"What should I get?" he asked, looking at the selections. Suddenly, his eyes lit up. "Do they have the one you're reading?"

"*Gulliver's Travels*?" She moved toward the section labeled classic literature. A moment's perusal revealed the answer. "*Ja*. Here."

"That's the one I want."

"Why's that?" she asked, handing it over.

"So we can talk about it." His posture straightened, as if he was shedding the weight of self-doubt. "All my life, I've seen folks reading books 'n stuff. But I never knew what they said. I wanted to ask, but then they'd know I was dumb. Didn't want them to think that, so I didn't say anything." He glanced at the selections he'd picked. "Now I'll know what the book says. And I can talk about it. Like a man who's got some learning about him."

Heart swelling with pride, Florene couldn't help but look up at him with admiration. His eagerness to explore the world of literature despite his educational handicaps was inspiring. His journey of discovery was just beginning, and she felt honored to be a part of it.

In that cozy space, she realized how much she wanted to be part of his world, to witness his triumphs and share his challenges. In his company, she found sanctuary from the harsh realities threatening to engulf her. Gil wasn't just her protector; he'd become her lifeline. She cared for him in a way that went beyond friendship, and she couldn't fathom a future without his reassuring presence.

Buffeted by the sudden rush of emotions, she dropped her gaze. Despite her feelings, it would be wrong to encourage his affection. She was still very much tangled up in a lot of trouble. Fleeing the source of her terror had only provided a fleeting illusion of freedom.

Dread coiled in the pit of her stomach. Carrying the burden of shattered dreams, she felt their sharp edges cut into her soul. Sooner or later, she would have to confront her abuser—and break the chains holding her captive to fear. As the father of her child, Zane Robbins would have to be dealt with. The legal and right way.

Until then, the forbidden allure of a new love taunted her, a reminder of the cruel hand of fate charting her path. Gil Kestler, with his tender smile and gentle touch, represented everything she craved—yet could not have.

Chapter Twelve

The family-style café, which exuded a rustic charm, welcomed all who sought to sit a spell and have a quiet meal. Wooden beams crisscrossed the ceiling, and simple, floral centerpieces sat on beautifully crafted tables surrounded by sturdy chairs. Patrons engaged in lively conversations.

"Thought everyone would enjoy being waited on for a change," Eli said as he took a seat. "It's so nice to get out and visit."

Nella adjusted Isaiah's travel seat, making sure the infant rested comfortably. "My *mamm* says she doesn't get to see us nearly enough. I'd love to live closer to my *familie*."

Letting the remark pass, *Mamm* brushed a hand across the gingham tablecloth. "The food here won't be as good as home-cooked."

"Now, *Mamm*, don't fuss. I'm sure the food will be fine." Walking around the table, Gil reached for the next chair. He tugged it out and gestured for Florene to take the seat. "Please, allow me."

"Danke." As she smiled, her gaze met his with

a hint of warmth. The borrowed frock she wore enhanced the flecks of gold lingering in her deep green eyes. A smattering of freckles adorned her complexion, giving her the look of an adorable waif. Her modest demeanor exuded a quiet grace.

Gil claimed the last chair. Unaccustomed to being out and about, he was acutely conscious of being on his best behavior. Their conversation paused as the waitress arrived, handing around menus.

"My name's Lilly," she said, patting her name tag. "Just holler when you're ready to order."

Eli waved her away. "Give us a few minutes."

"Of course," she murmured, moving on to serve other patrons. At the adjacent table, a lively group of *Englischers* were talking and laughing. They were engrossed in snapping pictures and recording videos on their phones.

Gil flinched when one participant aimed the lens his way. "Look at that giant," she snickered.

"They should put him in a circus," another retorted, eliciting more guffaws from the group.

Florene also noticed. The subtle tightening of her expression betrayed her discomfort. Seeking refuge in the menu, she angled it in front of her face. "That's so rude."

Gil couldn't agree more. Though it happened often, he'd never gotten used to the gawks and whispers whenever he ventured into town. The constant attention his stature drew only fueled his insecurities.

"Why do they always have to stare like that?" Eli groused. "I've half a mind to go over there and—"

"You'll do no such thing," *Mamm* warned. "Don't pay them no mind."

Embarrassed, Gil lowered his gaze. Why did people make fun of him? All he wanted to do was enjoy a meal with his *familie*. Was that too much to ask?

Laughter subsiding, the group turned their attention elsewhere. Their meal done, one man tossed out a handful of bills to pay the tab. Thankfully, the group departed without making any additional remarks.

Witnessing the exchange, the waitress stepped forward. "I'm so sorry about that, folks. I'll make sure the manager knows. They'll be banned if they come back."

Taking the lead, Eli nodded. "We appreciate that."

"Dessert will be on the house. Anything you want, just ask."

After the waitress departed, Eli sniffed with disdain. "*Englischers* are troublemakers. Don't like them, never will."

Mamm shook her head, a touch of sorrow in her eyes. "Folks just don't have any manners nowadays."

Gil snagged his napkin and spread it over his lap. "It's over and done. Just leave it be."

"Can we please enjoy our meal?" Nella whined, rocking Isaiah's travel seat. Mewling with discontent, the infant was getting fussy. "I'd like to have a nice afternoon."

Thankfully, the conversation turned to other topics. Then everyone was quiet as they took a moment to peruse the menu.

Florene's lips remained tightly pressed, her gaze on the plastic-coated menu. Now and again, she glanced around, as if expecting more trouble.

"It's okay," he said quietly. "No harm done."

A weak smile tugged her lips. "If you say so." Despite her acquiescence, a flicker of unease crossed her features again, betraying her inner turmoil.

Hunger gnawed, reminding Gil he hadn't eaten anything since breakfast. He opened his menu and recognized a few simple words, but most eluded him. The pictures helped him decide what to order. The offerings were mostly classic comfort foods.

Eli snickered. "You need help with that or are the pictures enough?"

Letting the verbal jab pass, he summoned the waitress.

Lilly returned, effortlessly juggling all requests. She scribbled down the order and flashed a smile before heading to the kitchen. Fifteen minutes later, she came back with their meals.

Before anyone could take a bite, Eli cleared his throat. "I guess now would be the time to share the news I have for everyone."

"Go ahead," Nella urged, clapping her hands. "Tell them."

Fixing his gaze on his younger brother, Gil braced himself. "What's that?"

Eli's grin widened. "Since it's *Mamm*'s doing, I guess I should let her say."

Mamm tightened her hold on her cane. "Eli took me to the courthouse today—" Turmoil etched in her expression, she drew a breath before saying, "I put his name on the deed and signed the quit-claim to give him the farm."

Gil felt his breath drizzle away. "All of it?"

Mamm reluctantly nodded.

"And that's how you want it to be?"

"Ja."

"Well?" Eli prodded. "What do you think?"

Gil didn't know what to say, so he chose silence instead. As for how he felt, he couldn't begin to process his emotions. It was akin to being slapped.

As she looked between her sons, *Mamm*'s shoulders slumped, as if under the weight of her decision. "I did what I thought was right." Emotionally blackmailed, she'd crumbled under the pressure.

Pleased as punch, Nella was bursting to share more. "There's more!" Reaching out, she clasped her *ehmann*'s hand.

Gil's pulse quickened, dread pooling in the pit of his stomach. "I suppose you're about to tell us."

Eli inhaled deeply before he spoke. "I've made a deal to sell the farm."

Mind racing, Gil struggled to grasp what Eli said. He'd poured his soul into the land of his fore-fathers, believing it would be a part of his legacy for generations to come. Now, everything he'd ever known had been yanked out from under him. He had nothing but a handful of memories and a heart heavy with sorrow. Betrayal cut deeper than any blade ever could.

"Well, it looks like you're not wasting a min-ute."

Mamm angled her chin at her younger *sohn*. "Eli, you never said a word to me about selling out." By the look on her face, the news had caught her completely off guard.

Undeterred by his deception, Eli pressed for-ward. "The land developer I've been talking with offered a fair price. I intend to accept."

Mamm's hackles rose. "Would this be the same fella that was asking to buy before your *daed* passed?"

"*Ja*. He left his card and said to keep him in mind."

Gil grimaced as the image of a well-dressed

man behind the wheel of a luxury vehicle flashed through his mind. At that time, folks had learned there were plans in motion to build a new campground and tourist center for travelers coming through to visit the nearby Dinosaur Valley State Park. Several property owners in the area had received offers, but most had refused the money. Land and heritage were far more important to farmers and ranchers than making a quick buck.

"As I recall it, *Daed* said it wasn't worth the consideration."

"I disagree." Crossing his arms, Eli refused to budge. "It was a sum I couldn't ignore."

"And we're all to go where?" *Mamm* demanded.

"We're moving to town," Nella answered, eager to share the plans they'd cooked up. "We've picked a nice corner lot to build on. Once it's done, we'll have a lovely *haus*—with modern appliances." Reaching out, she patted her mother-in-law's arm. "And don't think we didn't consider you, Almeda. We've found you a nice room with a few other ladies your age. Isn't that grand? You won't have to keep up that dreary old place anymore."

Gil flinched inwardly. The babbling little fool believed they'd done a good thing.

"The money won't last long if you've got plans like that. How're you going to make a living?"

"Niles offered me a job at the feedstore." Puffing up, Eli jabbed a thumb toward his chest. "I'll be training to be an assistant manager."

"And what's your *bruder* going to do?" *Mamm* demanded. "Where's Gil supposed to move his horses? And find a home?"

"Don't think I haven't thought about that," Eli breezed back. "I got Gil a job in the feed yard. There's always a need for a big man to do the lifting and loading. He can do that easily."

No, I won't.

Forcing himself to tamp down his emotions, Gil faced the grim reality of scrambling to find a new place—not only for himself and his mother, but also for his horses. However, his savings fell far short of what he'd need to purchase a new homestead.

"If that's what you want, Eli, then I'm glad you got it." Hardening his tone, he made sure his next words were clearly understood. "But you can leave me out of your plans."

"I'm doing this for all of us." Eli's voice trembled with emotion as he tried to defend his deception. "I've worked for a long time to pull this all together."

Refusing to be swayed, Gil calmly folded his napkin and laid it aside. Despite the setback, he refused to let despair take hold. He drew strength from the unwavering bond he shared with his Creator, knowing *Gott* would help him overcome the challenges.

"Your plans are nothing I'm interested in. I'll stand on my own." Even as he spoke, every fiber of his being strained against the rising tide threatening to consume him. The air crackled with tension as he battled the urge to unleash a torrent of words that would scorch everything in their path. But lashing out in anger wasn't the way *Gott* would want him to respond. Holding his temper would be the only way to get through.

The mountain might be high, but he'd prove he was man enough to conquer it. He had no other choice. The threat of losing everything he'd ever known loomed ominously. The only question that echoed was not *if* this heart-wrenching upheaval would unfold, but *when*.

Trust shattered, *Mamm* wasn't taking the news as calmly. "Eli, how could yo—"

She never had time to finish. Her son's betrayal was more than her heart could bear. Her face drained of color, and her complexion suddenly turned ashen. A sharp gasp escaped, followed by a desperate clutch at her chest. Then she collapsed…

Bright fluorescent lights illuminated the white walls of the hospital lobby. Huddled together on a row of uncomfortable plastic chairs, no one dared to speak above a whisper.

Head bowed, Gil sat with his hands clasped in silent prayer. Holding Isaiah in her arms, Nella wiped away tears, her eyes red from crying. Eli's usual snark was replaced by a somber silence. The weight of their collective anxiety filled the lobby with sadness.

Florene shifted in her place, gazing down the long hallway. The doors at the end remained shut. She stared hard, silently willing them to open and bring good news. But the medical personnel emerging kept passing by without pause.

The minutes ticked away. No news came.

Needing a distraction, she glanced at a stack of flyers arranged on a nearby table. Advertising details about the hospital's recent construction, the pages showcased images of state-of-the-art equipment.

Curiosity piqued, she picked one up. At one time, Burr Oak only had a small clinic. The nearest hospital was over a hundred miles away, and folks needing emergency care often didn't survive. The flyer detailed how the hospital was made possible through grants funding rural health care. Other community efforts, such as bake sales and auctions, filled in the gaps in support. As she read, a sense of pride welled up inside her. The Amish understood the importance of coming together for the greater good of all.

Lost in her reading, she barely noticed Gil raise his head. "The hospital's been a blessing," he observed quietly. "*Mamm*'s got a fighting chance, not having to go so far."

"I'm sure they're doing their best," she replied, placing the flyer back on the table.

"It's been hours." Rising, Eli paced back and forth, hands tightly clasped behind his back. "We should know something by now."

Anger flaring, Florene had no sympathy. To get what he wanted, Eli had betrayed his mother's trust. The stress of losing everything she knew and loved had undoubtedly contributed to Almeda's collapse. Shocked diners could only stare helplessly as the old woman was rushed away in an ambulance.

The pressure that had been building between the brothers had finally erupted.

Gil looked toward his brother. His eyes, usually warm and jovial, were now stormy with suppressed anger. "You know how much the farm means to *Mamm*. How could you take her home away from her?"

Eli's response was swift, his voice rising to match his brother's intensity. "I thought I was doing what was best for the *familie*."

"Best for the *familie*?" Gil scoffed bitterly. "If you mean for you and Nella, then you got what you wanted, I guess. But *Mamm* might be dying because of the stress you put her through."

"*Mamm*'s going to be fine," Eli said, as if speaking the words would make it so.

"I pray you're right."

"Nothing's going to happen to the farm overnight, anyway. It'll take a month for the quitclaim to process. Then another few months to arrange the move. By then, *Mamm* will be back on her feet."

Gil ratcheted to his feet, cutting off Eli's path. "*Mamm* doesn't want to sell out—and neither do I."

Eli came to a dead halt. "Then buy me out."

"If I had the money, I would. I'd give you every cent."

"But you don't," Eli countered, determined to hold his ground. "I've struggled long enough with that land. I'm tired of breaking my back, fighting the elements."

"Weather changes. The snow will help crops this year. Spring rains, too. *Gott* willing, you'll have a *gut* year."

"Too much is as bad as too little." Drawing back his shoulders, Eli crossed his arms. "I want a real job that pays a regular wage and puts money in my pocket."

Gil's resentment swirled like a tempest, raw and unyielding. "Guess money's all you think about," he drawled. "Awful funny how you had those papers ready for *Mamm* to sign. I'm sure you got her right to the county clerk's office as fast as you could."

"Mr. Blevins helped me have them drawn up," Eli admitted.

"The one buying the land?"

"*Ja*. All I had to do was get *Mamm* to sign them." A smirk teased Eli's lips.

"I hope you're happy," Gil said, backing away in disgust.

"I am. And I'm not sorry. I'm taking care of things the best I know how." Shifting his tactic, Eli spread his hands. "You got a chance for a better life, too. I've made the arrangements. Just take the offer."

"I liked things the way they were," Gil said, refusing to budge. "We had all we needed. No reason to ask for more. The Lord always provided."

Eli's gaze turned hard as his mask fell away. "Oh, stop! What's done is done. I'm not changing my mind about selling."

The tension thickened as the brothers argued, each grappling with conflicting points of view. The chasm between them widened, collapsing the fragile bridge of kinship.

Feeling a surge of protectiveness, Florene battled to keep silent. She wanted to speak up and condemn Eli for his selfishness—make him understand the pain he'd inflicted. But all she could do was sit and wait, her heart heavy with worry and anger.

A sudden cry pierced the lobby. It was the unmistakable sound of a distressed infant.

Florene's maternal instincts kicked in, and she turned toward the source of the crying. "Is Isaiah all right?"

"He's gone through his last bottle," Nella said, attempting to console her wailing *boppli*. "I have nothing else for him." Her eyes were rimmed with exhaustion and worry, the last few hours having worn her down. Despite the quibbling, she genuinely tried to get along with her mother-in-law.

"I'll take you to your *mutter*'s *haus*," Eli said, making a quick decision. "You can stay there and rest."

Nella nodded, tearfully agreeing. "All right."

"That okay with you?" Eli asked Gil. "The horse will need to be fed and watered, too, so I'll be delayed getting back." Shaking his head, he added to no one in particular. "Living in town, we wouldn't have to deal with the trouble of getting around in a buggy. There are better ways to travel nowadays."

"Stop complaining," Gil retorted behind a glower. "You got your way."

"Whatever," Eli sneered back.

Gil threw up his hands in a gesture of disgust. "Just go. I can't look at your face anymore. I might forgive you, but I'll never forget how you broke *Mamm*'s heart."

Eli claimed his wife and child. "Let's go."

"Ja." Nella leaned into him for support as he led her away. Isaiah's cries seemed to intensify, echoing the surrounding turmoil.

Florene couldn't help but shake her head as the couple made their way out of the lobby. Selfish and self-centered, they thought only about themselves.

A pang of recognition stabbed at her, memories of her past self mirrored in their obliviousness. But life had a way of humbling even the proudest souls. Time had not been kind, leading her through trials that brought her to her knees, stripping away her arrogance and replacing it with humility. Now, every step she took carried the fervent hope that she'd find a better path.

Sighing heavily, Gil sat back down. "I'm glad they're gone."

"Me, too." Florene reached out and squeezed his hand, offering solidarity. "Your mother is a strong woman. She'll be okay."

Another half hour ticked away. The wait continued.

And then, the doors down the far hall suddenly sailed apart. The sound of footsteps echoed on the hard tile floor. A tall, blond man dressed in a white lab coat approached.

"I'm Dr. Nelson," he said, greeting them solemnly. "Are you Almeda Kestler's family?"

"*Ja.* I'm her s*ohn.*" Gil stood, his eyes searching the doctor's face for any hint of what was to come. "How is she?"

"She had a mild heart attack," Dr. Nelson said, seeking to put him at ease. "But we caught it early and she's stable."

"*Ach*, thank *Gott*." Gratitude shone in his tired eyes. "Can we see her?"

Dr. Nelson shook his head. "We're preparing to move her out of ICU and into a private room. If you don't mind, we need to get her settled."

"Then she won't be able to go home soon?"

The doctor shook his head again. "She's tired and weak. I want to keep her a few more days for observation. Just to be on the safe side."

Gil shook his hand. "Then that's what we'll do."

"You look like you could use some rest yourselves," Dr. Nelson said before departing. "Take a break. A nurse will inform you when she is ready to have visitors."

Tears welled up in Florene's eyes as she listened to the conversation. Tense anticipation shifted to relief. "Almeda's going to be fine," she breathed.

Gil grinned. "Best news I've had all day." A smile crept past his exhaustion. "Right now, I'd say we need to take that break," he said, gesturing toward a glass door that opened into an adjacent break room designed for visitors. Inside, a row of vending machines stood alongside a drinks station. "I think we can get something to drink there. We'll be close by, so the nurse can find us, if need be."

"That would be nice," Florene said.

Standing, they made their way through the lobby, drawing a few curious glances from the

Englisch visitors. They hadn't taken more than a few steps when a voice from the past made her blood run cold.

"Florene…"

Blood pressure dropping to zero, Florene pivoted on her heel. A lanky figure loomed, not ten feet away.

As she recognized the man's rugged frame and piercing eyes, her breath caught in her throat. Her worst nightmare had suddenly turned into a chilling reality. And she was powerless to escape it.

His name spilled past her lips in a gasp. "Zane—"

Chapter Thirteen

Offering a crooked smile, Zane took a few steps forward. His unkempt hair fell in wild strands over his forehead and bloodshot eyes. Perspiration beaded his brow, and his pupils were dilated. The odor of whatever drug he'd recently smoked wafted off his wrinkled clothes. His sudden appearance was like a tornado sucking up the tranquility of the hospital.

"I've been looking for you, babe."

Lifting her hands, Florene took a cautious step back. "Stay away from me."

"Please, hear me out," he pleaded. "I didn't leave for very long. I came back, but you weren't there."

Images of that cold, vicious night flashed through her mind. "You left me in the middle of nowhere." She folded her arms protectively in front of her body.

"I didn't mean to. I wasn't thinking right, that's all." His expression was twisted, and movements erratic. Every sentence was punctuated by a wild gesture. "Come on. Please. Give me another chance."

A shiver clawed its way up her spine. His plea was the same as always. He'd say he loved her and promise to change.

But he never did.

Ever.

Summoning her courage, she glanced toward Gil. His presence nearby was a quiet but firm reminder of support and protection.

Speak your peace and walk away.

"No, Zane. It's over. I'm not doing this anymore."

"I've been worried…" he pleaded again, refusing to listen.

"How did you even know where to find me?"

"I got flagged on *BuzzMe* saying you were here, waiting for me to pick you up." Zane rolled his eyes. "I figured you finally got over being mad and had a friend message me."

Knots twisted Florene's insides. No, she hadn't. But she knew who might have. Burr Oak might be large in land size, but it was truly a small town, where lives intertwined like the roots of trees, impossible to untangle. Most everyone was on social media nowadays. It wouldn't be hard for someone to search and find a particular name. *Someone* who didn't want her around anymore.

Eli…

"It wasn't me," she declared. "But it doesn't matter. We're done. I've had enough."

Facade cracking, Zane refused to back off.

"You think you're just walking away from me?" Hand shooting out, he grabbed her arm. "You don't do anything I don't tell you." Grip tight, he jerked her forward, intending to drag her out with him.

Onlookers gasped, shocked.

"Someone call Security," one said in a voice loud enough to be overheard.

Panic surging, Florene pulled away. "Don't touch me!"

"Shut up!" he snapped, lunging again.

Gil stepped forward, blocking the grab. His sturdy frame towered like a mountain. "She asked you to leave her alone."

Zane's face contorted into a sneer. "Stay out of this, buddy."

Gil stood his ground. "The best thing you can do is move on."

Zane hesitated. Physically, he was no match against a man standing nearly seven feet tall. Stepping back, he pulled out an object tucked in his back pocket. With a flick of his wrist, the switchblade sprung open, clicking into place with a menacing snap. "Sure you don't feel so big now!"

Time seemed to freeze as Zane pointed his razor-sharp weapon at her. "A quick jab and it's over," he cackled. "No second chances, babe."

Without thinking twice, Florene positioned her body as a shield against the looming danger. If death had to claim a victim that day, she resolved it would be her. At the same time, she grappled with the devastating realization that her unborn child, too, would meet its end in this tragic exchange. Emotion surged like a tempest, yet her resolve remained unyielding, fueled by self-sacrifice and the desire to atone for her sins.

"Please, don't hurt anyone. I—I'll go with you."

Zane grabbed her arm. "About time you did what I said." Forcing her behind him, he brandished his weapon toward onlookers, daring the witnesses to act.

Fear-whitened faces gaped back. Everyone stood still, hardly daring to breathe.

"Don't do anything or someone will get hurt," he barked, pulling her with him as he retreated.

With a flash of grim acceptance, Florene prepared herself to face whatever divine judgment awaited her. The moment Zane got her alone, she was probably going to die.

Please be quick, she silently begged.

Someone else had other ideas.

Without hesitating, Gil surged forward with the unstoppable force of a steam engine. His momentum collided with Zane, sending the knife spinning to the floor with a metallic clang. The impact sent the smaller man stumbling back, but he recovered quickly, launching himself forward with determination. The lobby echoed with the intensity of the struggle.

Florene kicked the knife away, sending it skittering. "Please stop!" she cried, desperate to break through the chaos. She couldn't bear to see Gil harmed, nor could she stand the thought of her abuser reveling in the pain he caused.

"Get away, freak!" Zane threw a series of punches, but they had little effect.

Gil warded off the blows like pesky insects. "I've had enough." With calculated ease, he disrupted Zane's balance, causing him to stumble forward. Taking advantage of the momentary imbalance, he executed a deft maneuver, sweeping his leg behind Zane's and using his own momentum against him.

Zane crashed to the floor with a resounding thud. A snarl broke from his lips as he attempted to rise. "I'll get you!"

"If you say so." Gil's years of experience handling wild mustangs came into play as he smoothly flipped the smaller man over, expertly securing Zane's flailing arms with a practiced grip. With controlled force, he kneeled across Zane's legs, effectively immobilizing him.

Pinned, Zane tried to wriggle free. "Get off me!"

The flurry of approaching footsteps broke the tense standoff. Hospital security burst into the lobby. "Sheriff is on the way," a uniformed man said before pulling out his cuffs.

The other motioned for Gil to move away.

"We'll take it from here." He dragged Zane to his feet, attempting to take him into custody.

The looming threat of arrest spurred Zane to resist. With a burst of adrenaline-fueled strength, he wrestled free of the pair.

"I'll get even!" he seethed, voice laced with a raw intensity that matched the desperation in his eyes. "I'll make you all pay!" Propelled by a ferocity born of desperation, he evaded recapture. Sprinting around a nearby corner, he disappeared.

The next few hours vanished in a blur. The sheriff arrived, as did a crew of deputies and state police officers.

Ushered into the break room, Florene sat with law enforcement. All she knew was Zane was on the run, a fugitive from the law. Fearing he was armed with other weapons, law enforcement had mobilized every available officer in the area.

"I'll never understand what you saw in Zane Robbins," Sheriff Evan Miller declared. "The minute I heard he was back in town, I knew there'd be trouble."

Hands tightly folded in her lap, Florene sucked in a breath. "I thought I loved him."

Miller knowingly angled his head. "But?"

"After we eloped, Zane changed. He took away my phone, my money… Said I didn't need them, that he'd take care of me." Hardly able to speak, she dreaded the memories flooding back with painful clarity. "It got to where I couldn't go out or see anyone. He'd…" Anxiety jammed her throat, driving her into silence.

"I know it's hard, but I need you to tell me every detail, no matter how small."

Nodding, she forced herself to continue. "Zane would call me a stupid little Amish girl and tell me I was worthless." As she recounted the dark days she'd endured, her voice grew stronger, fueled by a newfound sense of determination. She described the bruises and scars that marred her skin, the nights spent cowering in fear, and the moments of fleeting hope that kept her going. "He made me a prisoner," she concluded. "I didn't ask for help because I was too scared. He threatened to do such terrible things."

"How long has Zane been using?" Sheriff Miller asked.

Unable to look the lawman in the eyes, Florene dropped her gaze. "Almost the entire time we were together." Disgusted, she wrinkled her nose. "He tried to get me hooked, too. But I never liked the way they made me feel."

"Gotten really paranoid, hasn't he?"

"*Ja*. He owes his dealers money. A lot." Fear curled around her spine, chilling her to the bone. "When he's strung out, he makes terrible threats…saying he'd hurt me and my *familie* if I ever left him."

"I feared you'd turn up dead somewhere,"

Miller murmured. "Guess we know now why you disappeared and cut all contact."

"It wasn't by choice." Forcing herself to continue, she finished with the night Zane abandoned her in the bitter storm. "I'd have frozen to death if Gil Kestler hadn't found me."

Sheriff Miller glanced toward the big man. Sitting nearby, Gil hadn't said a word.

"You could have been killed, facing down a man with a knife," he commented, jotting down more details for his report.

Gil's demeanor was inscrutable, betraying nothing about the trouble he'd been dragged into. "I knew *Gott* would take care of me, one way or the other." His faith wasn't just a belief; it was a way of life, woven into the very fabric of his being. He had no fear. He genuinely trusted that everything would turn out the way it was supposed to.

Miller eyed the larger man. "Well, I guess you are big enough to take care of yourself."

The barest trace of amusement lifted Gil's mouth. "Always have been."

"I'm so sorry," she said, her voice barely above a whisper. "I never meant to cause trouble."

"It's not your fault," Gil said, placing a reassuring hand on her arm. "You did nothing wrong."

"We'll make sure Zane doesn't hurt you or anyone else," the sheriff added. "Any idea how he knew where you were?"

Florene hesitated. She wasn't certain, but she suspected Eli had done the dirty deed. He knew her location, and he had the means. It might even be a criminal act, one that could land him in a lot of trouble. But without proof, she couldn't rightfully make the accusation. Someone else could have recognized her and tipped him off.

"I don't know." As it stood, a snarled web of secrets still threatened to unravel her world. Why add more fuel to the fire? She couldn't hide forever. If not today, Zane would have caught up with her another time.

It's over, she thought. If nothing else, it would spare Gil more grief. Eli's underhanded behavior had already given him enough to deal with.

The sheriff had no time to follow up. A deputy hurried into the break room.

"Sheriff, there's news—" His tone was mixed with urgency and disbelief.

"What is it, Jackson?"

"We got word from state troopers. They've been in pursuit of Robbins, and…and…" The flustered deputy paused, looking toward the civilians. "Should I go on?"

Miller nodded. "They have a right to know."

Florene's stomach twisted into knots. *Something bad happened.*

"Robbins totaled his car. He's gone. Emergency is on the scene now, clearing the wreckage."

The announcement hung heavy in the air. A

long minute ticked by, and then another. Sheriff Miller was the first to break the silence. "What happened? Was anyone else hurt?"

"Single car accident, near Rabbit Road," the deputy explained. "He took the curve too fast, went into the ditch, and flipped. Wasn't wearing a seat belt and he got thrown from the vehicle."

Florene gasped. Zane's threats still echoed in her mind, a promise of vengeance fueled by fury. "He was going to the ranch—" She dared not contemplate what might have happened if he'd made it to her *familie* home.

Instead of crushing her, the news lifted a burden she'd carried for too long. Her abuser, the man who had decimated her sense of self, was brought down in a blaze of poetic justice. Oddly, she felt no sorrow for his death.

The realization flooded her with conflicting emotions—grief for her own shattered dreams, anger at the injustice, and an odd sense of freedom. Her hand instinctively pressed against her middle. She carried a child she would raise alone, but free from his father's oppression.

A tear trickled down her cheek, and then another. They were tears of release. *It's over...*

"*Gott* was watching over your *familie*," Gil said quietly.

Sheriff Miller agreed. "Looks like the problem took care of itself."

Florene swiped at her face with steely resolve. "What happens now?"

The sheriff stood up. "Guess I'll inform his parents." A criminal, Zane was also a human being who had met a tragic end.

Struggling between disbelief and relief, Florene wiped away tears. "What do I need to do?"

"Go home," Miller advised. "Your sisters need to know you're safe."

"You think they'll forgive me?" As she remembered how they'd parted—in tears and anger—hesitation filled her. "I chose Zane over them. Just to prove them wrong."

"You made a mistake, but it doesn't have to be your whole life." Settling his hat on his head, the lawman offered a smile of encouragement. "Say you're sorry and get on with the business of living."

The day that began with such promise and hope had completely fallen apart.

As he attempted to process the tragic and tumultuous events, Gil's mind swirled with a blend of anger, grief and helplessness. The weight of responsibility pressed upon him like a mountain, threatening to crush his spirit. Everything he held dear was slipping away like grains of sand through his trembling fingers.

But the cruel hand of fate wasn't done with its relentless barrage. The woman he secretly cherished was the victim of a savage attack. Her ex-boyfriend, an *Englischer* with a history of abuse, had unleashed his temper upon her, leaving her broken in both body and spirit. Yet more news came in waves of horror. Zane had died in a car accident while fleeing police, a tragic end to a life marked by drugs and violence.

He ached with despair, his mind overwhelmed with thoughts of loss and uncertainty. His *bruder* had turned against him, stripping away his security and his very sense of purpose. The stark reality of impending homelessness loomed. His cherished horses, once a source of pride, were now a burdensome reminder of his uncertain future.

Bowing his head, Gil clasped his hands, feeling the rough calluses and scars that marked years of hard labor. *Gott*, he prayed silently, *I don't understand why all this is happening. I don't know how much more I can take. Please, give me the strength to endure. Help me protect the ones I love.* His prayers continued; for his mother's recovery, for Florene's healing and for guidance in the face of loss and upheaval.

Amid all the anguish, a sense of calm washed over him. It was as if a gentle hand touched his shoulder, offering comfort and reassurance.

Gaining strength, he drew a breath. "Guide my path, O Lord," he whispered. "And let *Your* will be done." Difficult as it was, he trusted *Gott*'s plan.

Done with his prayers, he forced himself to sit up. The doctor had promised someone would let him know when it was all right to visit *Mamm*. But so far, no one had come. If something had gone wrong, no one was saying anything.

Having taken Nella to her parents' home, Eli hadn't returned. In a way, Gil was glad his *bruder* had the *gut* sense to stay away. He had words for Eli, but he wanted to think some more before he said them. It could mean the difference between a reconciliation or a permanent division of the *familie*.

So much to think about. The beginnings of a headache rose behind his eyes, hammering at his temples. The *kaffee* he'd drunk curdled on his stomach, sending up a flux of acid. To say he felt awful would be an understatement.

But he wasn't the only one undergoing a difficult time.

Worried, Gil glanced toward Florene. Coat folded across her lap, she sat with her arms crossed protectively, hunched as if to make herself smaller and less noticeable. Her face was puffy, her eyes reddened from crying. Since receiving the news of Zane Robbins's passing, she looked shell-shocked. Numb.

Now that the danger was over, authorities had departed the scene. The hospital lobby returned to a sense of normalcy—though security guards made sure their presence was felt.

"Are you okay?"

Sniffling, she nodded. "*Ja*. I think so."

"I know it's hard, losing someone you cared about."

"I stopped caring a long time ago." A shadow darkened her expression. "I only stayed because Zane bullied me into believing I had no other place to go." Regret tugged her lips into a sad smile. "He told me I was stupid because I only had an eighth grade education and couldn't support myself."

Gil flinched. He knew from experience hearing things like that had a way of tearing down a person's self-respect. "It makes you feel bad."

"It's easy to believe it when someone's putting you down. I let Zane steal away everything, and then I had nothing. It's still that way. I have nothing." Shivering, she drew her arms tighter around her body. "Nothing at all."

"That's not true. You have your *familie*, your sisters. It's like Sheriff Miller said. You can go home now." Even as he spoke, the words tore a little hole in his chest. He didn't want Florene to leave. However, considering the snarl Eli had created, it was probably better if she didn't get tangled up in the fallout.

Longing mingled with doubt in her gaze. "I want to…" A soft sigh pressed past her lips. "But I wonder if I can?"

"Why not?" he asked.

"Before I left, I accused everyone of being against Zane. I just couldn't see they were telling the truth. He always made me think it was everyone else's fault for the way he acted." Shaking her head, she sighed again. "How could I be so blind?"

"We always want to see the best in folks. Like how *Mamm* always wanted to see the best in Eli. But he fooled her and now—" he glanced down the long, cold hallway "—she's fighting for her life." Pain suddenly clenched his insides. "I don't know if she'll be able to survive if Eli does sell out."

A woman dressed in a white uniform slipped through the double doors, her thick-soled shoes padding softly on the ceramic floor. "Mr. Kestler?" she asked, searching among the people waiting for news of their loved ones.

"That's me." Anxiety thudding, Gil stood.

The nurse turned with a warm smile. "You can see your mother now."

"Danke." His tense shoulders relaxed slightly. "How is she?"

"She's a little groggy from the medication," she replied, motioning for him to follow "You can sit with her a little while. Just remember not to say anything upsetting."

Gil nodded, grateful. "I won't."

Florene didn't rise. "You go ahead. You've got

enough on your hands without adding my drama to the mix."

"*Mamm* will want to see you, too."

Hesitation flickered in her eyes. "You sure?"

"*Ja. Mamm* thinks of you like a daughter."

Amusement tugged at her fine mouth. "Sometimes, I wish she was my mother."

The nurse led the way, guiding them down a series of corridors. "Mrs. Kestler is there," she said, pointing toward the private room.

Gil nodded. *"Danke."*

Entering the room, he approached his mother's bedside. She lay peacefully, her eyes closed. Stray locks of gray hair brushed her forehead. He took her hand in his, feeling the warmth of her skin and the steady rhythm of her pulse.

"Mamm?" he whispered, his voice breaking at the sight of her so frail. "I'm here. You're going to be all right."

Eyes fluttering open, *Mamm* stirred. A weak smile crossed her lips. "Gilead…" Her murmur was barely above a whisper.

Tears welled up in Gil's eyes as he leaned in closer. "How are you feeling?"

"Oh, I've been better. I'm just sorry I made a mistake."

"Don't think about it. It'll be fine."

"Eli's selling," *Mamm* said, tears filling her eyes. "We'll have no home."

Worried she'd stress herself into another attack,

Gil moved to calm her nerves. "We'll get another place, just as soon as I can manage."

"I don't want to move," she moaned. "I want my *haus*." She clutched at him with trembling hands. "Silas must be rolling in his grave. That land belonged to his great-*grossdaddi*. It wasn't ever meant to be sold, but kept in the *familie*."

"I guess Eli had other ideas."

Remorse shadowed *Mamm*'s expression. "I shouldn't have let Eli twist things the way he did. It wasn't fair to you."

"You were doing what you thought was best. I can't blame you for that. I know you believed Eli would be more likely to stay if he owned the farm outright."

Mamm shook her head. "I took what was rightfully yours," she said softly. "I see now how much I've hurt you, and how much I've lost."

"You haven't lost anything," Gil said, giving her hand a reassuring squeeze. "Heard Jeb Zook's parcel is for sale, just north of town. A couple of acres would be enough to start over."

"That old place?" *Mamm* clucked her tongue. "It'd take a lot of work."

He gave her an encouraging smile. "We'll do just fine."

Mamm nodded weakly, and then her gaze settled on Florene. "It's *gut* to see you, dear."

Florene hurried to her bedside, taking her hand

gently. "I couldn't leave without knowing how you are."

Confusion dimmed *Mamm*'s face. "Leave?"

"Florene's going home," Gil explained gently. "Back to her *familie*'s ranch. That fella who was giving her problems passed away—in an accident. He won't bother her again."

Surprise pursed *Mamm*'s lips. "I was hoping you'd stay, and let Gil help raise your *youngie*," she b lurted.

Astonishment gave Gil a hearty kick. He'd had no idea. "You're having a *kind*?"

Shame flushed Florene's cheeks. Without a word, she nodded. The look on her face revealed the dread that she'd be rejected.

Silence hung heavy between them, the reality of her confession hitting like a thunderbolt. Gil felt a surge of conflicting emotions—torn between his feelings and the shock of the unexpected news. The woman he secretly adored, the woman he'd hoped to court one day, was carrying another man's child.

"You don't have to raise it alone," he blurted without thinking twice. "I'd help. Just like a *daed* would."

Her eyes widened, and her lips parted slightly. "I couldn't ask you to take on more burden than you're already carrying."

"I want to," he said simply.

"I haven't known what to do," she confessed in a rush. "I don't even know if I want to keep it."

"A *boppli* is a blessing," *Mamm* whispered from her bed. "A gift from *Gott*."

Gil's pulse raced. A surge of protectiveness and determination filled him. Decision made, he boldly claimed her hands.

"Florene, I love you," he declared. "If you'd give me a chance, I'd be there for you and the baby." More than words, it was a promise to stand by her side, to support her in whatever trials lay ahead, and to love her unconditionally, despite the challenges they would surely face.

"A new *boppli* in the *familie* would be such a delight," *Mamm* said, pleased.

Tipping her head, Florene locked her gaze on his. *"Nein,"* she breathed. "You're so sweet and so kind, but I can't accept."

Disappointment gnawed. Having a *familie* was everything he'd dreamed of—and nothing he'd ever have. "All I'm asking for is a chance." His appeal was woven with the earnestness of a man who had found his truest desire.

Florene's expression faltered, a mixture of regret and sorrow clouding her features. "It's not you," she said, gently uncoupling her hands from his. "It's me." Stepping away, she unpinned her white *kapp*. Slipping it off revealed the shaggy, choppy cut beneath. "I can't accept because I can't be Amish again."

Dismay filled him. It was a bittersweet realization—that sometimes, love alone was not enough to bridge the chasm of expectation and obligation. "I thought you wanted to come back to the church."

Fresh tears spilled down Florene's cheeks, indicating the grip of conflicting emotions. A symbol of faith and tradition, the head covering slipped from her grasp, dropping to her feet with a soft hush. Its fall echoed the fracture in her beliefs.

"I…" Her voice quivered, and her body trembled uncontrollably. "I don't believe in *Gott*—and I don't know if I ever did."

As if unable to bear the weight of further confession, she turned suddenly and fled.

Chapter Fourteen

The hospital hallway was a blur as Florene stumbled away from Almeda's room, tears streaming down her face. Her confession hung heavy in the air, a weight she'd been carrying for weeks. Now it threatened to crush her entirely.

She loved Gil Kestler. No doubt about it. Somehow, without even meaning to, she'd fallen head over heels for him. He was the best thing that had ever happened to her, and she wanted to marry him. With all her heart. But he was Amish. And he deserved to wed a *gut* Amish *fraa*, a woman as devout as he was.

She was not. Giving up her beliefs, she'd walked away. Sure, she could pretend, mouth the right words, say the right prayers. But if she didn't believe them, didn't *feel* them, then her entire life would be a meaningless sham.

He deserves better than me.

Rounding a corner, she pressed forward. She didn't know where she was going, only that she couldn't stay there, couldn't face the judgment and the whispers that would surely follow. And she couldn't look that wonderful, caring man in the eyes and keep on lying.

She had tried to find *Gott*. And had found nothing but silence.

Gasping for breath, she found herself in front of a set of wooden doors. The sign read Chapel. With nowhere else to turn, she stumbled inside. She needed a moment. To sit. To think. To clear her mind.

The chapel's interior created a peaceful atmosphere conducive to reflection, prayer and solace. Muted colors dominated the decor, with pastel hues of blue, green and beige contributing to the soothing ambience. A modest crucifix served as a focal point for worship. The atmosphere of serenity was a stark contrast to the noise of the beeping monitors and hurried footsteps echoing in the corridors outside. A comforting space, it invited all and turned away none.

As she sank onto a bench, her heart ached with despair and uncertainty. Others found solace in the Bible's teachings. But now, faced with the reality of her situation, she felt lost and alone.

Clasping her hands, she closed her eyes tight. "Please, Lord, show me something—anything— to tell me You're there."

Silence.

And then a gentle voice interrupted her thoughts. "May I sit with you?"

Startled, Florene looked up to see a man standing nearby. He appeared to be in his later years, with hair that had receded to reveal a smooth, balding crown. Spectacles perched upon a gently creased face, framing eyes that held a depth of understanding born of decades spent in service. His white collar and dark clothing marked him as a member of the clergy. His hands clasped a worn Bible. But it wasn't just his age that commanded respect; it was the way he carried himself, the aura of gentle authority that seemed to envelop him.

"I—I guess so," she stammered.

"You look like you could use some company." Without blinking an eye, he settled beside her, his presence a comforting weight in the silence. "Happy to meet you. I'm Pastor Michael." He offered his hand. "And you are?"

"Florene," she offered timidly.

"Amish?" he asked, eyeing the simple cut of her dress. She no longer had the coat Almeda had given her. She'd laid it aside in the hospital room and hadn't reclaimed it before departing.

"Was," she corrected, shaking her head. "Not anymore."

"Would it be intrusive if I asked why?"

She hesitated, reluctant to speak. Her past was ugly. Awful.

Sensing her hesitation, Pastor Michael patted her hand. "I'm here if you want to talk," he said.

"Sometimes, the greatest comfort we can offer is simply to be present. To listen, to hold a hand, to share a prayer."

"*Danke*, Pastor. I—I don't even know where to begin."

"The beginning always works."

Hope glimmered. Pastor Michael had offered a willing shoulder. One she needed so very desperately to lean on.

"I fell in love with an *Englischer*. I left everything I knew because I wanted to be with him."

Pastor Michael nodded. "I see. I understand the Amish are expected to marry within the community. I imagine that would have been a disappointment to your family."

"*Ja*. It was. I haven't spoken to my sisters for three years."

"That's quite a long time."

"It's all my fault," she admitted, voice trembling slightly. "I chose a monster I had to leave for my own safety."

The pastor blanched as he listened. "Was that the man who caused the trouble earlier?" He shook his head. "Terrible, terrible thing."

"It was." Tears welled in her eyes as she recounted the terrifying moments when Zane had threatened her life. Security and police had intervened, but the memory of his last violent outburst lingered. "Thankfully, no one was hurt," she finished. "The only one Zane killed was himself."

Lifting her hands, she covered her face. Despite their estrangement, guilt continued to hammer away at her fragile psyche. "He's dead because of me."

"It wasn't your fault. Evil often wears many masks," he said solemnly. "But you are strong, stronger than you know. God has a plan for you, and it does not include suffering at the hands of such a cruel man."

Tears welled up again. It wasn't just the shame of being an unwed mother that gripped her now; it was the knowledge that she no longer believed in any divine being.

"I thought I could find happiness outside our community, but I was wrong," she whispered, her voice barely audible. "I lost myself trying to fit into his world."

"And now you want to go back to yours?"

She nodded.

"Is there a reason you can't?"

"I—I'm sorry to say it…but I don't think *Gott* exists."

"Why is that?" he asked.

"So many bad things happen," she blurted. "Not just to me. I deserved what I got. But other people, *gut* people who never harmed anyone. Their lives just fall apart."

"If it helps, I can tell you that doubt is a part of the journey for all of us," he said. "It is in these moments of questioning that we become tangled in the snare of darkness. Evil works hard to lure us away from the light."

Tears welled up in Florene's eyes as she struggled to find the right words. "I have prayed, seeking answers and guidance, but the silence has been deafening. I've tried to redeem myself, but I don't feel *Gott*'s presence in my life. If I said I did, it would be a lie. Because of that, I can never go back to being Amish."

"But you want to?"

"*Ja.* With all my heart. But to be baptized, I would have to give a statement of faith. I can't go back to my community if I don't truly believe in Christ."

Instead of horror, concern and compassion tinged his expression. "Florene, my dear child, your honesty is courageous."

Discouraged, she let her hands fall limply in her lap. "All my honesty means I'll be alone for the rest of my life. No *gut* man will have me, and I can't marry in the church."

Pastor Michael inclined his head, peering over the edge of his glasses. "Is there someone special?"

"I met someone recently, Pastor," she admitted without revealing any names. "I'd marry him, but he can't be with someone who doesn't share his faith. And I can't ask him to leave it because it means so much to him."

Pastor Michael sighed, understanding the gravity of her situation. "It pains me to see a heart torn in two."

"I'd give anything to start over, to believe as strongly as he does." Shoulders burdened with sorrow, she believed her life had diverged onto a path she'd be doomed to walk alone. She was bereft of all hope, adrift amid a crashing sea. The undertow threatened to drag her under, and there was no land in sight.

I'm beyond salvation, she lamented silently. Maybe that was why *Gott* remained silent. Perhaps the Lord had given up.

The pastor nodded understandingly. "Why do you think you can't?"

"I don't know. If only *Gott* would speak up!" Pushed to the edge of frustration, she lifted her hands, clenching her fists. "I need a sign, something undeniable."

Pastor Michael chuckled. "I'm afraid our Lord's handiwork isn't always found in the extraordinary. Faith isn't always about certainty."

"But how do I know what I'm supposed to believe in is real?"

"You don't. Being a believer is not about having all the answers or seeing miracles on demand. It's about trusting God's plan and finding joy in the everyday blessings He bestows upon us." His voice cracked with emotion as he spoke, revealing the depth of his own experiences and struggles.

She looked up, her gaze searching his for answers she hoped he could provide. "Is it really that simple?"

Pastor Michael smiled warmly. There was no judgment in his gaze, only a profound sense of connection. "Doubt isn't a sign of weakness, but a testament of our humanity. Faith is a lifelong journey of growth, challenges and moments of divine revelation. Take each step with courage and trust, for the path may twist and turn, but it always leads us closer to the Lord."

A tear slipped down her cheek. "I've sinned so much," she confessed, wiping it away. "Am I beyond redemption?"

"God's forgiveness knows no bounds," he replied, offering a kindly smile. "All He asks is that we come to Him with a repentant heart."

"How do I do that?"

He smiled warmly. "Would you like me to lead you through the prayer?"

"*Ja*, please."

Closing his eyes, he lowered his head, "Lord, I repent of my sin," he began, his hands clasped together in front of him. "By faith, I accept You into my heart."

Bowing her head, Florene echoed his words. "Lord, I repent…"

As she prayed, a sense of peace washed over her, filling the void that had lingered within her for so long. In that moment of surrender, she felt warmth spread through her being—a rekindling of the spirit waiting patiently for her to rediscover it. A profound sense of peace enveloped her. The confusion clouding her mind melted away, replaced by a calming certainty.

"I know that I know that I know," she murmured, her voice filled with conviction. The hallowed stillness she'd once feared became a comfort, mantling her in a newfound strength. Stilling the voice of self, she'd finally learned to listen, to let *Gott* speak.

In that moment, she knew she was not just a survivor, but a warrior. A warrior who had faced her fears and emerged stronger, ready to welcome a future filled with hope and healing.

Just like that, Florene was gone.

Bending, Gil claimed the prayer *kapp* she'd abandoned. He picked it up gently, feeling the weight of it in his hands. It was a tangible reminder of her absence and the stunning blow of her rejection. Remembering what she'd said, he felt as though the ground had shifted beneath him. His beliefs were not just a part of his life; they were the very foundation of his existence.

But that didn't stop him from loving her.

"I meant what I said," he murmured into the void she'd left behind. "Every word." His mind reeled with sadness, confusion and a profound sense of loss.

"I know, *sohn*," *Mamm* said from behind. "You've got a *gut* heart."

"No one seems to want it." Swallowing hard, he sank into the chair beside his mother's bed. "No one seems to want me." Throat tight with emotion, he looked at the abandoned *kapp*. His fingers traced the stitching of the coarse linen material. Memories of Florene's gentle manners and the warmth of her smile lingered like fragile whispers in the corners of his mind. How could he reconcile his feelings for her with her lack of faith? How could he find solace in a world where the woman he cherished didn't share his beliefs?

"She's had so much trouble, you can't blame her for being confused," *Mamm* said softly, her voice weak but full of wisdom. "She was away a long time. Adjusting to being Amish again would be a hard road to ask anyone to walk."

"I suppose you're right."

"Considering what she's been through, a couple of weeks isn't near enough. She needs time to heal, in her mind and her spirit."

"I want to help, but I don't know how." Torn between duty and desire, he felt a flood of emotions surge through him. The teachings of his community stressed the importance of tradition, family and the Plain way of life. Yet, his heart yearned for a woman who didn't belong to the faith.

A thought prodded. He wasn't baptized. He'd

made no vow to the church and could walk away at any time.

Should I?

It wasn't an easy choice. He'd have to weigh the consequences and consider what he had to lose. Florene made him feel alive in a way he'd never known. And he couldn't ignore that.

He closed his eyes, attempting to imagine a future with her—a small house nestled in the countryside, *youngies* playing in the yard, the satisfaction of enjoying a meal after a long day of labor.

Other thoughts crept in, darkening the pleasant vision. He saw the faces of his *familie*, his friends, his neighbors, their disapproving whispers and judgmental stares. He heard the echoes of his *daed*'s voice preaching about the sanctity of their way of life. Could he turn his back on everything he'd been taught?

Indecision gnawed. He knew that whatever choice he made would come with sacrifices. To stay meant denying the love that consumed him. To leave meant forsaking his heritage.

As though she knew his thoughts, *Mamm* spoke up, offering support. "If you want to be with her, you have the right."

Gil lowered his head, staring at the *kapp* in his hands. In a generous act, the woman who had given him life was willing to sacrifice dearly held beliefs for his happiness. Desire was a powerful thing. But he also knew what the Bible said.

A believer cannot be yoked with unbelievers.

Shaking his head, he tucked the *kapp* away. "I was born Amish, and I intend to die that way. I can't go against my beliefs."

"I knew you'd choose the Lord," *Mamm* said. "But don't turn away from her, or take away your friendship. Florene's fallen, but she could find her way back."

Hope flickered. "Then you're saying there's a chance?"

Mamm managed a smile. "You're not marrying the girl today. Tomorrow may be different. She's trying to start over, but she's stumbled, is all. Belief is a journey, not a destination. Show her acceptance and forgiveness—the way others have when you've fallen."

Gil nodded, a sense of peace settling over him. "I'll do that."

Just then, the nurse entered. "I'm sorry to interrupt, but visiting hours are over for the night."

"*Ja*, I understand," he said, rising from his place.

The nurse bustled around, checking to make sure all was well. "How are you feeling, Mrs. Kestler?" she asked, checking *Mamm*'s pulse and temperature.

"I've had better days," *Mamm* sniffed, not entirely comfortable with the poking and prodding. "I'll feel better when I get to go home."

"If everything's good with your tests, Dr. Nelson may consider releasing you tomorrow," the nurse said. "Tonight, you need to get all the rest you can." Checking her watch, she turned to Gil. "I'll give you another minute, but then you've got to go." Stepping away, she busied herself updating the notes in *Mamm*'s chart.

"I'd rather sleep in my own bed," *Mamm* groused, trying to get comfortable. "If I've got one when I get back." Tears suddenly welled in her eyes and her voice began to tremble. "Eli's probably already sold it out from under me."

Gil brushed a hand across his mouth. The problems Eli had created still needed to be dealt with. He intended to have a word with his younger *bruder*, just as soon as time allowed. The fact that Eli hadn't returned to the hospital told him all he needed to know. Eli was trying to avoid the fallout of his selfish actions. But that was Eli. Always skipping off without paying the piper.

Sucking in a breath, he steeled himself for the battle yet to come. "I promise, I'll fix this, *Mamm*. I'll find a way to make things right."

"From the way Eli was talking, he's set his mind to it," *Mamm* grumbled. "Nella's been pushing to move into town. He'll give her what she wants to keep the peace."

"It isn't right. If Eli wanted to sell the farm, it should have been a decision we all agreed on."

Mamm's gaze clouded. "I guess I'm the one who made it. Eli kept moaning, and I gave in."

"I know you were just trying to look out for Isaiah."

"That little one, he's my heart." More tears escaped, trailing down her cheek. "Losing Annabella…and then your *daed*… I didn't know how I'd go on. Then Eli got married and Isaiah was born. It gave me hope again."

The nurse discreetly cleared her throat. "I'm sorry to interrupt, but you have to go," she said. "You can come back in the morning."

Gil nodded. "I'll be at the inn down the street." Going back to the farm so late in the evening didn't make sense. Eli had also taken the buggy, giving him no way to get around. Rather than pay a taxi for the long ride home, it would be better to rent a room in town.

The nurse nodded. "I'll make a note of that in case we need to get in touch."

He leaned down to press a kiss on his mother's forehead. "Get some rest. I'll be back tomorrow," he said, adding a silent prayer for her comfort and peace.

"Go find Florene," *Mamm* said sensibly. "She can't be wandering around all night by herself."

"I will."

Mamm gave his hand a final squeeze. "The

Lord knows the desires of our hearts. If something is meant to be, it will happen in its own time."

Gil looked at his mother, her face etched by years of hard work and devotion to their way of life. *"Ja,"* he mumbled. "It will."

Picking up the coat Florene had left behind, he exited the room. He paused and surveyed the corridors with a sense of bewilderment. The hospital was like a maze, winding every which way. He followed one hallway, and then another.

A woman carrying a clipboard smiled kindly. "Looking for something?" The tag pinned to her suit indicated she was a support staffer of some sort.

"Have you seen a *fraulein* in a blue dress? She might have come this way, about ten or fifteen minutes ago."

"The Amish girl?"

"Ja."

The woman pointed. "I believe I saw her in the chapel talking to Pastor Michael."

Thanking her, Gil hurried toward his destination. The double doors were open, inviting anyone to enter. A slender figure sat in the pews, conversing with an elderly gentleman.

Relieved, he hastened down the aisle. "Florene."

She turned, eyes widening in surprise. "You found me." She broke into a radiant smile.

"I was worried." He held out her coat. "You forgot this."

She accepted his offering. "I didn't mean to scare you. I just needed someone to talk to." Her eyes shone as she turned to her companion. "Pastor Michael has been helping me sort through things."

Gil nodded at the pastor. "I appreciate that."

Pastor Michael smiled warmly. "I'm always happy to lend an ear." He stood and picked up his Bible. "I hope you won't think I'm abandoning you, but I have other duties to attend."

Florene smiled, clasping his hands warmly. "*Danke*, Pastor, for helping me find my way."

Pastor Michael beamed. "I was just a humble guide. May God bless and keep you as you continue your journey." A moment later, he'd departed.

Florene turned back to face Gil. "Oh, Gil," she exclaimed, her gaze sparkling with light. "You won't believe what happened."

"I'd like to hear," he said, claiming the space beside her.

"The pastor helped me find my way back to *Gott*." With a trembling voice, she recounted how Pastor Michael had listened to her without judgment, and then gently guided her back to the path of belief. "He showed me that *Gott*'s love is always there, even when we feel lost," she said, her voice filled with gratitude. "I feel like a weight has lifted. I feel…whole again." Her face glowed as she spoke. She meant what she said and believed it.

A surge of gratitude filled him. "Praise the Lord. I was so worried when you ran away. I didn't know where you were going or what you would do."

"I didn't either, but I do now." Drawing a breath, she held his hands. "If Bishop Harrison will allow it, I want to be baptized in the faith."

Gil's heart skipped a beat. Baptism was a significant step in the Amish community, a public declaration of one's commitment to the church and way of life. "You mean that?"

She inhaled deeply, as if gathering courage. "There's something else," she continued, her voice trembling ever so slightly. "I'm ready to give us a chance." Charged with emotion and meaning, her words filled the air between them.

A lump welled in his throat. He'd never dared to hope she might have feelings for him. "You and me—together?"

"If you still want to give it a try, I'm willing," she whispered. "I want my *boppli* to grow up the right way. With a real *daed*."

"I'll do my best for both of you." And he meant it. The little one was wholly innocent, deserving of safety, shelter and stability. Earthly fathers were meant to serve with humility, and he would feel no shame.

Smiling, she murmured, "I know you would."

Their gazes locked with a longing that transcended words. Everything else faded away.

Without a word, Gil pulled her close, never wanting to let her go. Their lips met. Filled with promise and devotion, it sealed their commitment to face the future.

Together.

As they pulled away from each other, Gil felt a guffaw bubble up from deep inside.

"What's funny?" she asked.

"Just remembered I've got nothing to offer a *fraa*." Happy as he was, reality would soon paint a stark picture of their future together. "Not even a roof to cover your head."

Eyes widening, she laughed, too. "It doesn't matter," she declared and gave his hands a reassuring squeeze. "As long as we're together, I believe *Gott* will bless us with everything we need."

Chapter Fifteen

Going home was the hardest thing she'd ever done.

As the van rattled down the graveled road, Florene's heart raced with a tumult of emotions. Three long years since she'd abandoned the ranch, chasing love and dreams that now lay shattered in her past.

The prodigal returns, she thought, remembering the parable of the lost son. The Bible story of a journey from prideful rebellion to humble repentance uncomfortably mirrored her own life. More than a physical homecoming, her arrival was a spiritual one. The echoes of past mistakes reverberated in her mind. Would her sisters welcome her back—or would she be met with cold stares and judgment?

She mentally steeled herself for what lay ahead. "You think they'll want to see me?" She'd made a vow to set things right, and somehow, she'd find a way to make it happen.

Gil reached for her hand, offering a reassuring squeeze. "I know they will."

Desperate to find calm, she attempted to shift her focus away from her nervous thoughts. The last few days had blurred together, a whirlwind of menacing conflicts and crushing emotions. Grappling with the twists and turns, she'd prayed for strength and guidance. Thankfully, the drama had settled down, allowing her the time to tend to the most important task of all.

"Almost there," the driver said, following the directions given by the GPS.

The ride continued. Rolling hills dotted with mesquite trees and scrub brush whizzed by. Barbed wire fences corralled the wide, open plains. Longhorn cattle roamed within, their massive frames casting striking silhouettes against the snowy backdrop.

Then the homestead came into view, a harmonious and unique fusion of Amish architecture and traditional Western influences. Following the circular drive, the van pulled to a stop in front of a rambling two-story house circled by majestic burr oak trees, its whitewashed exterior was adorned with handcrafted shutters. A winding stone path led to the back entrance. Sheltered by overhanging branches, a swing set and other play items waited to deliver hours of fun. Across the drive, the barn stood, doors ajar to reveal a glimpse of the livestock. Cowhands engaged in their daily chores paused to assess the newcomers. A few waved but were otherwise engaged in the business of keeping the operation running.

"Would you like me to wait?" the driver asked.

"We'll be awhile," Gil answered, paying in cash.

Florene wavered before opening the door. She'd sent word they'd be coming. "Should we have him stay? In case they don't…"

"It'll be fine," Gil said, unfolding himself from the cramped space. He wore a simple suit, and a wide-brimmed hat shaded his face. His demeanor was one of assurance. Choosing discretion, they'd agreed not to reveal their feelings for each other right away. They planned to take time and court properly.

Calmed by his strong presence, Florene prepared for the worst. She need not have worried. The back door flew open, and a barrage of smiling faces spilled out. Gail and Levi Wyse. Rebecca and Caleb Sutter. Amity and Ethan Zehr.

"You're here!" Gail exclaimed, rushing forward with outstretched arms. Amity and Rebecca followed, enveloping her in a circle of hugs.

"I'm so glad you're safe," Rebecca cried, hugging her a second time.

"Evan Miller told us everything," Amity said, getting right to the point. "I can't imagine how scared you must have been."

"It's a blessing it's over and you're safe," Gail added.

Levi extended a hand toward Gil, greeting

his old friend. "Almost didn't recognize you, all shaved and dressed up."

Gil laughed, taking his hand. "Thought I'd best look decent."

The cheerful group chatted for a few more minutes. The air echoed with laughter, tears and the sweet sound of reconciliation.

"I'm about to freeze," Rebecca declared, rubbing her hands against the chill. Ever the mother hen, she ushered everyone out of the cold.

Crossing the threshold, Florene searched out every detail. Some things had changed. Others had not. The heart of the home, the kitchen was a scene of timeless simplicity.

The smiling faces of nieces and nephews waited to be greeted. The oldest, Seth, stood nearly six feet tall. Sammy, bouncy and full of energy. Jessica, sweet and rosy-cheeked. Amity's stepchildren, Liam and Charity, had grown, too. She'd also added twin *boi*s to the mix, identical in every way. Rebecca proudly introduced her and Caleb's foster child, a precious little girl of about two years old.

"We've been approved for adoption," she shared with an excited laugh.

"In a few more months, she'll be ours," Caleb added with a smile.

"There's so many!" Florene exclaimed, happy to return the hugs. "I've missed you all more than words can say."

"What matters is you're here," Gail said. "And we can all be together again."

With the brashness of innocence, Jessica ran up to Gil. "A giant!"

A smile tugged Gil's lips. "*Ja.* I guess I am."

Rising to the tips of her toes, Jessica held out her arms to be picked up. "Make me big, too."

Gil hesitated, glancing toward the little girl's parents. "Is it okay? I don't want to scare her."

Levi laughed. "*Ja.* Of course."

"It's her favorite game," Gail added, smiling.

Bending, Gil swooped Jessica up. "How's that for standing high?" he said, lifting her toward the ceiling.

Jessica giggled. "I fly!" the four-year-old squealed.

That was all it took for the entertainment to begin. The smaller children gathered around, eager to get in on the fun. Amity's twins giggled with delight as each got a turn. Towering and robust, eyes alight, Gil interacted happily with the children.

Watching him, Florene couldn't help but feel a surge of pride, knowing that beneath his strong exterior lay a soul as gentle as a lamb. Her gaze grew misty again.

Danke, Gott, for giving me this man.

"Are you okay?" Gail asked, laying a hand on her arm.

"*Ja,*" she sniffed, swiping at her eyes. "I'm so happy to be home. To be safe again."

Levi frowned. "If I'd known Zane was mistreating you, I'd have done something right away."

"It's over. Done. I'm ready to put it behind me and move on." Why make everyone feel bad? Someday she would share the details. Today, however, was not that day.

Bustling around, Gail reached for her percolator. "I'll put the *kaffee on* and we'll visit."

Moving to the counter, Rebecca uncovered a platter. "I made cinnamon buns. Baked fresh this morning."

"There'll be roast beef and mashed potatoes for supper." Amity gave an anxious look, wringing her hands. "You will stay, won't you? Both of you."

"Never met a meal I didn't like." Grinning, Gil patted his stomach. "Hope you got enough to feed a big fella like me."

Tiny as a hummingbird, but full of sass, Amity looked him up and down. "Why, I'll need a stepladder just to serve you."

Laughter burst forth, painting smiles on everyone's faces. Tending the smaller ones, the older teens took them in hand so the grownups could visit. *Kaffee* served, the group settled down.

"Miller told us about Almeda," Levi said after downing a bite of his dessert. "I pray she's well."

"*Mamm*'s fine," Gil drawled back, parceling out details in his usual way—barely to not at all. "Eli's plan to sell to that land developer upset her, but we'll get through."

"That fella's been making offers all over the place." Brow furrowing, Levi frowned with disapproval. "Came here, too, but I turned him down. Heard through the grapevine he's having issues with financing, so wonder where the money's going to come from?"

"I suppose Eli will find someone to pay the price he's asking."

"Shame he's yanking it out from under you," Ethan Zehr said, joining in. "*Daed* was lucky to get the old Klatch place at a *gut* price when they were selling."

Giving the conversation half an ear, Florene allowed her thoughts to wander to the land her *familie* owned. Beyond the homestead lay acres of rolling hills and verdant pastures. Part of that was supposed to be hers. "I was telling Gil I had inherited some land. Is that still so?"

Busy at the sink, Gail answered. "Of course. You have one hundred and fifty acres to do with as you want. Oh, and you have your percentage of the profits—as we all agreed when Levi and I took over the ranch." Wiping her hands on a towel, she rummaged through a drawer. "This is your share." She handed over an envelope.

Unfolding the pages, Florene scanned through them. Years of deposits were listed, all made in her name. She gaped as the overall figure sank in. "I didn't think it would be this much."

"The herd is growing, and we've run in the

black for years," Levi said. "Everyone gets a share after the cattle go to auction."

"We all agreed after *Daed* passed," Amity said, reminding her of the bargain. "The eldest would run the ranch, and we would all split the profits."

It was all too much, too fast.

Overwhelmed by the surprise, Florene felt the room around her blur and sway. Flushing hot, she closed her eyes, willing herself to stay conscious. *Oh, my...*

Caleb stepped in. Catching her arm, he guided her to sit down. "How far along are you?"

Dismay scorched her cheeks. "How did you guess?" Passing out wasn't the way she'd planned to break the news.

Caleb returned a knowing look. "I'm a doctor. And I know that glow."

Surprise lifted Gail's brows. "You're with child?"

Florene nervously clasped her hands. "Close to four months." No reason to lie. She wouldn't be able to hide the fact much longer.

Worried, Levi scraped a hand across his bearded face. "Is it—?"

"*Ja*. Zane is the father." She glanced toward Gil, worried how he might react. He didn't blink.

"Did he know?"

Hesitating, she shook her head. "*Nein*. I never told him."

The group exchanged glances, their expressions a mixture of sorrow and relief. Relief that she'd escaped an abusive partner, but sorrow for the difficult path that lay ahead.

"What are you—" Gail broke off, unable to finish.

Florene stood firm. Having made up her mind, she intended to stand behind her decision. One hundred percent. "I thought about giving it up. But I'm not. I'm keeping my *kind*."

Rebecca nodded her support. "It's the only sensible thing to do."

"It's not a shame. Plenty of little ones appear during *rumspringa*," Ethan Zehr said, referencing that time when Amish youths ventured out to explore life outside the Plain community.

"Oh, tell me you plan to stay?" Gail immediately began making plans. "We'll get your room ready, and you can move right in."

Amity placed a comforting hand on her shoulder. "You won't be alone. We'll all help you get through."

"I know you will." Gathering her courage, she went on. "As soon as I can, I want to speak to the bishop—about coming back to the church."

"That's the best thing you've told us today," Levi declared.

Rebecca beamed with happiness. "*Gott* is truly *gut*."

Handkerchief in hand, Amity dabbed her teary eyes. "We prayed through three long years for your salvation. Bishop Harrison will surely welcome the news, too."

"I hope he will forgive the way I yelled at him the last time we spoke," Florene said, embarrassed to recall the *sturm und drang* proceeding her departure. The church elder had done his best to counsel her against choosing a man like Zane. Determined to have her way, she'd made a fool of herself.

"Bishop Harrison believes in forgiveness," Gail said. "He'll allow you a chance to make amends."

"I want that more than anything. I don't belong in the *Englisch* world. I never want to be part of it again."

"After you're baptized, I pray you'll meet a *guter amischer mann* and settle down." Rebecca playfully waggled a finger. "Like I always said you should."

Levi jerked a thumb toward Gil. "Might want to consider this handsome fella," he teased behind a grin.

A flicker of mischief sparked in Gil's eyes. "Don't know if I'd be the kind she'd want," he drawled, offering a quick wink.

Smiling, Florene gazed back at her beloved. "I'd be a fool not to."

And she meant it. With all her heart.

Epilogue

A few years later...

Florene bustled about her kitchen, working to prepare the midday meal. She moved gracefully, her plain dress swishing softly as she chopped fresh vegetables and kneaded dough for home-made bread. The woodstove filled the kitchen with a comforting glow, casting soft shadows on the worn wooden floors and the simple, yet sturdy, oak furniture. She hummed a hymn under her breath, her movements purposeful and efficient.

So that she could work, her mother-in-law had taken over the care of her *sohn*. Nearing his second birthday, Jeremiah was walking and using basic words. To entertain the child, Almeda sat by the hearth, delighting in his giggles as she played peekaboo with him using an old quilt. The little boy's chubby cheeks dimpled with laughter.

"*Ach*, he's such a jolly one," she declared, bundling Jeremiah into her arms for a long hug.

Rocking the toddler, she whispered, "You are my sunshine."

Jeremiah squealed, and the game continued.

Florene smiled as she watched the two play. "You spoil him so."

"Can't help it," Almeda said. "Never met a child so filled with joy."

"He takes after his *daadi*." And he did. As far as she was concerned, Gilead Kestler was Jeremiah's father. And she wouldn't have it any other way.

Returning to her cooking, she scraped the vegetables into a pot simmering with thick chunks of beef. The dough was covered with a lightly floured cloth, and then set aside to rise. A glance at the clock told her lunchtime was near. As she set to fixing her *ehmann*'s lunch, she couldn't help but reflect on the journey that had brought her such contentment.

Marrying Gil had been a dream come true. Not that it had all been so easy. Their path to be together was a rocky one, taking time and patience to navigate. They'd waited until after Jeremiah's birth to wed, opting for a small ceremony. Some folks hadn't approved, urging Bishop Harrison to deny their plans. Ever forgiving, the bishop had overruled the objectors. Long weeks of counseling and guidance were required before she could make her statement of faith. When her time had arrived, she'd spoken about her experience, recounting the journey that had brought her back to the community. As promised, Gail, Rebecca and Amity had supported her every step of the way, as had their husbands.

Baptism had cleansed her soul, preparing her for the spiritual rebirth to come. She now lived a humble life, in harmony with *Gottes wille*.

Thank you, Lord, for all you've given me, she thought, silently praising her Savior. Difficult as things had sometimes gotten, she'd never been happier. Life was perfect, in every way.

Face suddenly going hot, she paused to open the window above the sink. Handsewn, white curtains billowed gently in the cool breeze, carrying the sweet scent of wildflowers in from the garden outside.

She pressed a hand against her forehead. Her skin was warm, and damp with perspiration. She'd suffered identical symptoms carrying Jeremiah and knew the signs well enough.

I'll have to say something...

Making up her mind, she packed the food she'd prepared into a basket. A hard worker, a big man like Gil required a hearty meal to tide him over until dinner. She'd made his favorites—thick ham sandwiches and, to satisfy his sweet tooth, chocolate brownies loaded with walnuts. Iced tea would wash it all down.

"Would you keep an eye on Jeremiah while I take this out to Gil?" she asked. "I'll only be a minute. Then I'll come back and put him down for his nap."

"Be happy to."

"If he wants a snack, there's apples and peanut butter."

"I'll make sure he eats." Rising from her chair, Almeda led the toddler into the kitchen. "Are Nella and Eli still coming for dinner?"

"*Ja*. Far as I know."

Now that the drama over the land had been settled, Gil and Almeda were working to repair their strained relationship with the couple. As fate would have it, the deal to sell the farm had crumbled. A loss of key investors had brought the proposed development to a standstill.

Unable to carry the homestead on his own, Eli had had a change of heart. In a moment of humility and redemption, he'd attempted to make amends by deeding Gil his fair share of the property. Between the two of them, the brothers had agreed that Gil would assume ownership of the old farmhouse. In return, Gil would help Eli build a home better suited to the needs of his *familie*.

Though it wasn't a perfect arrangement, it made life tolerable for all concerned. Slowly the wounds of betrayal began to heal. Having let desire and envy blind him to what was truly important, Eli was striving to be a better man. He'd sought counsel from the *Leit*, humbly asking for guidance for himself and his *fraa*. As his commitment grew stronger and the seasons turned, the crops in the fields flourished once more. And when the pair came to visit, Isaiah loved tumbling around with his younger cousin. Together, the two little *boi*s were like peas in a pod. Soon, more *youngies* would join them. Nella was expecting, as were Gail and Amity. Her *familie* tree was deeply rooted and growing stronger.

Almeda had, of course, stayed in the old *haus* she loved, right where she belonged.

Basket in hand, Florene headed outside. Passing the old barn and corrals, she admired the sturdy new structure they'd recently built. A stable, still smelling of fresh pine, filled the space. The money she'd inherited had helped pay for the construction. An investment in their future, she didn't regret the expense.

Inside, Gil labored diligently, taking care of his horses. The herd was a reliable source of income. To make extra money, he'd also begun offering full boarding services, plus a stall with full turn out to pasture. For those who had a busy schedule, it was an ideal arrangement. To help with the driving and other sundry chores, he'd hired Donny Reese to work part-time. Now sober, his *Englisch* friend was attending church regularly and cleaning up his own property. Donny had even mentioned that he was in touch with his daughter and proudly showed the pictures of his grandson that Mary had shared.

Once again, Gil had been right. Everyone deserved a second chance.

"Time for a break," she called, setting the basket down on a nearby picnic table perched under the shady branches of sturdy trees.

Gil broke into a smile. "I was just thinking about a bite," he said, setting aside his pitchfork and taking off thick leather gloves. He walked over and leaned in to kiss her.

Florene eyed him from head to foot. During their courtship, he'd kept himself neat. After their nuptials, he'd relinquished the razor, proudly growing out his beard. The scent that clung to him was a rich blend of perspiration, saddle soap and the earthiness of hay—a testament to the hard work and passion he poured into running his business.

"Not until after you've had a bath this evening," she teased, playfully wrinkling her nose and pushing him away. The gentle giant did indeed resemble a shaggy beast. But beneath his rough exterior beat the heart of a handsome prince. She adored him just the way he was.

Laughing, Gil scraped his palms down the front of his shirt. The elbows were covered with colorful patches, and his trousers frayed at the hems. "Suppose I do look a little grubby." Taking a seat, he dug into the basket. "My favorite," he said, unwrapping the sandwiches before taking a hearty bite.

Watching him, Florene felt another wave of

nausea twist her stomach. Standing on the other side of the table, she steadied herself and pulled deep breaths to calm her racing heart.

He immediately noticed her distress. "Is something wrong?"

Despite the lightheadedness, she managed a nod. "I… I have news."

His worried gaze searched hers. "Is it bad?"

The secret she'd been keeping bubbled out. "I'm going to have a *boppli.*"

Gil's rugged countenance softened with a mixture of awe and tenderness. Grinning wide, he stood and rounded the table in a few quick strides. "I've prayed so long for this day." Lifting her off her feet, he twirled her around in a joyful dance.

Florene laughed, her heart overflowing as the man she loved held her close. Arms circling his neck, she offered her lips. "I think this is where we kiss."

"Thought you said—"

She grinned. "Changed my mind."

Delighted to oblige, he claimed her mouth with his. As they pulled away, their eyes met, each conveying an understanding that words could never fully capture.

"Ach, liebchen…" Lowering her to the ground, he pressed his open palm against her middle. "You've made all my dreams come true." He brushed his lips against her forehead in a tender act of adoration.

Florene smiled up at her husband. Their love had produced a new soul, a testament to the beauty of their bond. "*Our* dreams," she murmured, snuggling back into the safety of his strong arms. Laying her head against his chest, she closed her eyes.

Leading her through dark valleys, the Lord had lifted her from the depths of despair, granting her not just health, but profound healing and unwavering hope. Yet, above all these blessings, He had sent a man worthy of her deepest affection—to cherish, to honor and to love.

Surrounded by the sounds of the farm and the security of her beloved's embrace, she knew their lives would be forever entwined.

As for being Amish...

It wasn't so bad, after all.

* * * * *

Dear Reader,

I can't believe I'm up to the fourth book in my Texas Amish Brides series. It's taken some time, but I was finally able to sit down and write Florene's story.

If you've followed the Schroder sisters, you know Florene is the youngest, and a rebel whose path has been the most challenging. Her story is a testament to her stubbornness and strong will. In her quest to prove everyone wrong, she's strayed far into dangerous territory. Her wayward actions have brought her to the brink—one that could very well threaten her life and that of her unborn child. But God, in His infinite wisdom and mercy, has a plan for His lost sheep. He sends Gilead Kesler, a towering man with a heart as big as his stature. Gil's unwavering faith, even in the most trying circumstances, becomes a beacon of hope and redemption for Florene. I pray her journey back to the Amish will touch your hearts the way it did mine when I was writing it.

If this is your first visit to Burr Oak, I hope you will check out the other books in the series. Do visit me online at www.pameladesmondwright. com. You can browse all my Love Inspired releases—and discover what's coming next. While you're there, don't forget to sign up for updates, sent straight to your inbox! I love hearing from readers, and you can contact me by regular mail, too, at PO Box 165, Texico, NM 88135-0165

Bless you all!
Pamela